DAMAGE

Also by Eve Ainsworth

7 Days
Crush

DAMAGE
EVE AINSWORTH

SCHOLASTIC

Scholastic Children's Books
An imprint of Scholastic Ltd
Euston House, 24 Eversholt Street, London, NW1 1DB, UK
Registered office: Westfield Road, Southam, Warwickshire, CV47 0RA
SCHOLASTIC and associated logos are trademarks and/or
registered trademarks of Scholastic Inc.

First published in the UK by Scholastic Ltd, 2017

Text copyright © Eve Ainsworth, 2017

The right of Eve Ainsworth to be identified as the author
of this work has been asserted by her.

ISBN 978 1407 16429 8

A CIP catalogue record for this book
is available from the British Library.

Printed and bound by CPI Group (UK) Ltd, Croydon, CR0 4YY

Papers used by Scholastic Children's Books are made
from wood grown in sustainable forests.

1 3 5 7 9 10 8 6 4 2

This is a work of fiction. Names, characters, places, incidents
and dialogues are products of the author's imagination or are used
fictitiously. Any resemblance to actual people, living or dead,
events or locales is entirely coincidental.

www.scholastic.co.uk

To my mum for her strength and kindness.
And for always telling me to put my best
foot forward. I'll keep trying.

I went back. I went back and I opened the door.

Just behind me the storm was swelling. Heavy rain whipped against my back, clawing at me, trying to drag me back into its cold grip. My thin coat was already soaked right through and clung against me like a wet, useless flannel. The empty bins rattled with the force of the gusts and the gutter poured water against the wall, a relentless, murky waterfall, spilling out on to my shoes.

It was nasty, unforgiving weather that refused to end. This was meant to be the start of summer, but it might as well have been the depths of winter.

I edged through the door and into the room beyond.

The smell hit me first. Deep, dark and filthy. It settled in my throat and made me want to gag. The light was poor. All the curtains were drawn, as if the house was closing in on itself. Entering the room was like stepping into a rotting piece of fruit with its juices slipping down my throat and into my nostrils, making it hard to breathe.

I walked through the next door, gently pushing

it aside. The TV was so loud that the sound was distorted. Canned laughter bounced off the walls, mocking the scene in front of me.

Laughter. So much laughter.

I wanted to block my ears. I wanted to run.

But I didn't.

I had a question to ask.

CHAPTER ONE

Everything feels different now.

As I stand at my bedroom window, looking out at the same view I always have, I can't feel the same about the usual stuff. I mean, nothing much has actually changed in fifteen years. I'm still looking out on the same drab car park. There's always a car or two nestled in the corner, usually bashed, battered and abandoned. And right now, Dad is there again, standing in the centre of the tarmac, taking yet another delivery for the pub. He is clutching his clipboard and laughing with the driver as he checks off the barrels. He stands, legs slightly spread, belly hanging over his tightly belted waist. From up here I can see the bald patch that he tries so hard to disguise. He still likes to think he's one of the lads. He loves it here. He always has.

But I no longer see what he does.

I would have done, once. Before. The old me would have done. I'd have been out there with him, messing around. Winding up the driver, Terry, for being ten minutes late. Laughing and joking and acting like I didn't have a care about anything. I was his daddy's girl. That's what they all said, because we were so alike.

They were so wrong. I'm nothing like him. Not any more.

Not that anyone can see it – to the outside world I'm still that same girl. But inside is where it counts, and inside is where I've changed.

The wall beyond the cark park is stained and crumbling. The garden it protects is spilling over, trying to escape – giant weeds and tendrils peeking through the holes in the brick. I can just about make out the top of a giant trampoline. Once you'd have seen the McKenzie twins leaping up and down on it, making contorted shapes in the sky, but they are both too old for that now. I expect the poor thing is rusting into the ground. It's certainly lopsided; I think the brick wall is the only thing keeping it upright.

Over on the right are the garages. The one facing me has been smashed in and the door hangs loose like a broken tooth. I don't think many people keep cars in them anyway.

Further along from the garages is the curve of the local shops. The newsagent, the corner shop, the hairdresser. I used to plot my route over there, planning how long it would take to run to Del's corner shop and buy my weekly sweets. Most days I could make it in two minutes if the road was clear, some days longer if Del decided to strike up a conversation – usually about something dead boring, like school. He's old now, so his sons run the shop, and they don't bother talking to anyone. You're lucky if you get a smile from them.

Behind the garages is the main sweeping street of Washington Road and the skatepark beyond –

the park that used to make me buzz inside, just thinking about it. Standing here, looking out, I would dream and plan, imagining what I could do next time I was there. That park means everything to me. I guess it always will.

I press my nose against the glass and picture the road behind the trees at the back of the garages. If I squint I can make out the outline of the chimneys, tiny identical stacks – little fat men nestled in the greenery. I wish I could take myself there. To his house. I wish I could teleport myself through glass and sky and be there, outside that cracked, tumbledown terrace. I want to lay my hands on that rough dried-out wood and push the gate. The gate that always got stuck.

But at the same time I wish never to be there again.

I already miss him so much.

This is me now. Confused. Stupid and damaged. Everything is ruined. Someone has dimmed the lights inside of me and it's awful. I'm a deserted building full of rattling ghosts and memories.

I need to escape.

But I have no clue how.

It's later.

Mum is standing at the bar, shrugging off her jacket to reveal her delicately cut black dress. An orange juice is clutched in her slim, tanned hand, and she is laughing. She never drinks alcohol, not even at Christmas; I've never seen her take so much as a sip. Beside her, Dad is chatting loudly to one of the regulars, Craig, and laughing at a joke that is bound not to be funny at all. The people that come into the pub are always full of wisecracks and most have punchlines wetter than the leaking barrels in the cellar. But we have to laugh. Part of our job is to keep other people happy – make them feel important and special, even if it's only for a minute or two. Mum is particularly good at pasting a grin on her face; it's part of her uniform, and – I rarely see her without it. Now Dad makes a joke, but unlike most of the regulars he's actually funny. Mum laughs the loudest and wraps her arms around him. He bends down and kisses her on the head.

It's almost sweet. Almost.

I hate being down here, but it's either this or sitting upstairs alone in the flat listening to the constant noise. You can never escape. The pub clings to you wherever you go.

I am sat in the far corner of the pub, the rough velvet of the seat rubbing against my bare legs. The table is sticky and everything around me stinks heavily of beer. I have my "Don't even think about coming near me" face on, which keeps most people away. Beside me, Amira is texting – Freddie, obviously, but that's OK. She's managed to resist for most of the evening. I'm just glad she came. It's a sign of a best mate that she'll rock up to our mouldy old pub to keep me company when I'm grounded. Again.

"Freddie sends his love," she says, placing her phone down in front of us, a little smile on her face. "He hopes you'll make it down the park tomorrow."

"Of course I will – if they let me." I scowl.

"You'd think having an opinion was the worst crime in this world."

Amira frowns a little, which briefly spoils her perfect little face. Where Amira is just petite and pretty I'm the total opposite: long, gobby and loud.

"You *were* a bit out of order," she says, her tiny hands stroking the wooden table nervously. "I don't think your mum deserved the mouthful you gave her."

I glare at Amira and then look away. If anyone else had said that, I would've gone crazy, but Amira knows she can get away with most things. She's known me a long time now.

"I only called her a bitch. I could've said much worse," I mutter. I know I sound sulky and hate myself for it.

"How's it been? Is it still weird since. . ."

"Since Granddad died?" I snap. I don't mean to. I soften my voice. "It *is* weird. It's not like—"

I feel a shuffling nearby and look up to see Dad standing next to me. He thumps a drink on the table; the lemonade dribbles over on to the worn beer mat. His thumb rubs at the liquid absently, dragging the liquid into the wood of the table.

"You OK, Gabs?" he asks. "I got you this. Thought you might need something. You hungry yet?"

"I'm all right."

"You need to eat. I'll fetch you something from the kitchen." He glances over at Amira. "What about you, sweetheart? Want anything? I've a lovely pie on the specials list."

"No thank you, Mr Matthews," Amira answers politely. "I'll be eating with Mum later."

Dad still stands there. I can feel him shifting awkwardly, like he wants to say something else. I know he won't; Dad has never been big on words. Or anything too deep. But I kind of love him for that – he's like a big clumsy bear.

"Hadn't you better look after the bar?" I say to him.

"I just wanted to see if you're OK—"

"Why wouldn't I be?"

He sighs. "Yeah. Why wouldn't you be?" He

ruffles my hair and I cringe. I hate it when he does that. I'm not five. "It's your mum I worry about," he says, lowering his voice. "She's not as tough as she makes out. You really upset her earlier – you know that? Aren't you ready to talk to her yet? Apologize?"

I glance over at her. She's leaning over the bar, giggling with a customer. She looks OK from where I'm sitting.

"She needs us right now, Gabs," he says softly.

I shrug. That is as much as he's getting from me.

"You need her too," he says, more firmly now.

I look back over at her. She is still laughing. Her eyes catch mine and for a second we look at each other. It's like time freezes for a moment, before she turns her head and moves away from the bar.

I think it's pretty clear I'm the last thing she needs.

Me and Mum are complicated; that's the only way I can explain it. Some people are lucky – they have close relationships with their mothers. I don't. It's that simple. And it's been that way for as long as I can remember. Dad, yeah. We're OK. We have fun, give each other space, make each other laugh. But Mum – I don't know. Somehow it always seems to go wrong.

Amira doesn't get it. It's one of the few things that annoy me about her, how she just doesn't seem to understand. She looks at my mum's carefully made-up face and designer clothes and thinks that she must be cool and fun to be around. And yeah, maybe she would be fun – if she wasn't related to me.

I know it seems like I'm being harsh, but I'm not. Honestly, I'm not. I know Mum feels the same way. This is not one-sided. I am not the bitch daughter here. There's this ... wall between us, this force field that prevents the two of us from getting too near to each other. Dad says we're like magnets repelling each other. It must be pretty hard for him, I guess. He's either stuck in the middle trying to sort it out, or, more usually, ignoring the problem completely and hoping it'll go away.

I think we both stopped trying a long time ago, which is sad in a way, but that's just how it is. Some people aren't meant to get along, are they? You can't make these things work. If we forced it much further, one of us would snap.

The evening passes in a blur. Amira is with me for a bit. We were meant to be making plans for the summer holidays but she spends most of the time updating me on life with Freddie. Eventually she leaves to have dinner with her mum, and slowly the pub empties. I watch Mum and Dad go about their work for the evening, watch them see out the last of the punters and start to cash up the till, and I can feel the familiar dread in my stomach, that uneasy feeling that we are about to have another row. I always know when it's about to happen. It's like a change in the air, an electric current circulating between us. We are both charged up and it only takes one of us to spark. One small thing, usually the tiniest, stupidest thing, and we blow up. BAM!

Right now, Mum is doing her act where she talks to me via Dad. She knows it does my head in. It's like she's trying to wind me up on purpose.

"If she thinks I can forgive her that easily this time around, she can think again," she says, her voice deliberately soft and silky. She is rubbing down the bar, her long fingernails pinching the cloth, dragging it across the wood – probably leaving marks in the varnish. It's making a noise, slightly high pitched, that drills into my ears. I don't flinch though. I keep my face neutral, staring right at her like I don't care what she thinks.

"It's not good to let these fights drag on," Dad is saying gently. He looks at me and gives a little smile, nodding now, trying to encourage me to speak.

"She needs to learn. . ." Mum continues, voice firmer now. "I'm fed up of all the abuse. I don't deserve it! She's out of order."

Dad's voice is still smooth, trying to drip comforting words into the fire. "I'm sure—"

"She never thinks of me! She—"

Of course it never takes long for me to finally snap.

"I am here! I do actually exist!" I dip into her sight, waving my arms around for effect. "I know you'd like to think that I was out of your life, but I'm still here. I'm still alive."

"Gabi! That's not fair," Dad says.

Mum just sighs. She looks at me sadly, like I'm the biggest disappointment in her life. "I know you're here."

"Well then, stop talking like that. It's crazy."

"Have you apologized yet, Gabi?" Dad asks.

"For what?"

Mum jumps in – she can't resist. "For calling me a – what was it? 'A stuck up, skinny-arsed bitch'!" She smiles sweetly. "I think I'm remembering it right."

My cheeks sting. "I was just angry."

I think back to the night before, to what set it all off. There were questions I had, questions about Granddad. Things I deserved to know. Things she wouldn't tell me. And when she refused point-blank to talk about him, I flipped.

"It was out of order," she snaps.

There is nothing for it but to apologize; she'll never believe she's anything but in the right, and I can't bear for Dad to look so worried. He doesn't deserve any of this.

"I'm sorry." I say it as calmly as I can, trying to keep the edge out of my voice. Trying to stop more words from tumbling out – they are there, on my tongue, but I swallow them back, hating their taste. The bitterness seems to stick in my throat. I want to say more, of course I do. But it's pointless. I know that by now.

She nods. A tiny smile settles on her lips. She *does* look perfect, like one of those carefully made-up models you see on TV. In that moment I can see what Amira sees, what everyone sees – except no one else bothers to chip beyond the surface. No one knows what goes in that head of hers.

She sees I'm still staring at her and flinches slightly; her hand reaches up to stroke her hair.

"Thank you," she says. Then she turns and walks away. Tall. Calm. Composed.

She is nothing like me.

It's funny the things I remember. Memories clutter my mind like rolling marbles; sometimes it's hard to focus on just one. Even when I want to, want to more than anything. I replay everything again and again, like a film. But the images get jumbled, the words get lost, and as time passes my confidence in what I can accurately remember weakens. I hate that. I hate that the most.

It's all slipping away.

And I want to remember EVERYTHING, especially the early days. Those days when everything was better. When *he* was better. Why can't I keep those memories safe, locked away? Why do they keep escaping?

The few I have left are precious. I only have to catch the smell of earth on the air, and I'm back there next to him, aged about five, digging out worms with my fingers – dropping them down on to his tatty white trainers, watching them squirm and curl against the rubber. I can hear him humming tunelessly far above me, a song that sounds so beautiful to my small, sharp ears. Or remembering our trips to the park, when he would always push me too high on the swing and make me squeal as my tummy looped inside out.

We had so many good times.

I remember the first time he came back into our lives. I was only little, about four I think. It was certainly before school. There was a stranger in the bar, sitting with Mum and Dad. I was playing in the corner and Mum had come over and taken my hand. She'd seemed different that day, really nervous – and she held on to me far too tightly, her grip pinching the skin on my hands.

"We need you to meet someone," she'd whispered as she led me over. "Someone special."

I'd looked towards this man sitting at the table, dressed in a scruffy leather jacket and faded jeans. He looked a bit like a scarecrow – all tatty and mismatched, but with a beaming smile.

He winked at me and crinkled up his nose. He reminded me of a character on children's TV. Somebody warm and friendly. But still somebody that I didn't know. A stranger.

"This is my dad. Your granddad," mum said softly.

I stared at him, a bit confused. Mum had never mentioned her Dad before. I hadn't even known he'd existed until that moment.

He stood up, all formal. "Gabi. I'm so pleased to meet you!"

I think I was a bit scared, despite his friendly eyes. I remained glued to Mum's trouser leg, gripping the material tightly between my fingers. She gently stroked my hair. "It's OK, lovely. It's OK. Don't be shy."

Dad wasn't saying much. He kept tapping the beer mat on the wood of the bar and eyeing my granddad suspiciously, like he did with the occasional customer in the pub that he didn't like much. "It'd better be OK this time," he said, talking to Granddad like the rest of us weren't there.

Granddad was still smiling, but he sat down again quickly. "You don't have to believe me, but it's true. I'm a changed man. I've got a lot to prove to this family, but I'm back to do things differently."

I didn't know what he meant. "Back?" I asked. Back from where?

"Granddad has a house down the road now," Mum said. "So we'll be seeing a lot more of him." There was something funny in her voice – something hopeful and young.

"And I'm going to make it my mission to be a good granddad to you," he said. He looked at me and then he looked at Mum.

"You owe me that at least," Mum said quietly into my hair. The breeze of her breath tickled my ears.

I looked back at my granddad, who just grinned at me again. A sweet man with a nice smile and twinkly eyes. My tummy leapt with happiness. I had a granddad.

CHAPTER TWO

I wake up with the fist punching my stomach. The ice-cold feeling deep inside of me that sparks chills down my spine and radiates through my entire core. The memory. The realization.

Granddad's dead. It wasn't a dream.

He's gone.

My thoughts are buzzing constantly, like bees inside my brain. They buzz inside my skull at first and then move deep down into the pit of my stomach, where they'll settle for the rest of the day. Some people wake up feeling good, excited about the day ahead. I guess I used to be one of them. I lie here, looking at the light dancing across the ceiling, wondering how long I can get away with not actually moving at all.

It's never silent in our home. Downstairs I can hear the soft drone of the hoover, the scrape of chairs being moved around. Dad will have the radio on; he'll be reading the paper, leant up against the bar while Mum cleans around him. They'll talk. They'll discuss the day ahead, or gossip about the regulars. They might even talk about me – Mum, with the lead draped over her arm, moaning about my behaviour whilst ramming the hoover hard against the skirting boards. If only I was dust or dirt, she could suck me up and forget about me. Another problem solved.

I shut my eyes again – my lids are heavy and my head feels sludgy. I could go back to sleep, but it would be shallow and restless. I'd probably wake up with a worse headache and the buzzing would still be there.

Nothing stops it.

Thoughts are swishing inside me. Bad thoughts. A heaviness that is kind of difficult to describe;

it's as if I'm carrying all my tears inside me. I can feel the weight of water pulling at my stomach, straining the linings. It's sickening. It makes me want to puke.

Slowly I get out of bed. I take a gulp of stale water and head for the shower. The day is bright already and I try and convince myself that this is good. A long day in the sun, at the park. A day's skating is what I need. I stretch out my limbs; I force them to wake up, to move as they should.

In the bathroom I run the shower warm as always and step inside. I tip cool gel on to my skin, Mum's expensive stuff. The smell is too sweet and almost makes me gag. I rub the foam into me, dragging the thick suds across my body – leaving long trails, slimy and rich.

The water feels good. It's waking me up, drumming against my skin, seeping into my muscles. At last I can feel something that isn't dread. Reaching forward, I turn the dial, listening to the hiss as the boiler kicks in. It's hot now, really hot. I turn my face towards it, blinking in the mist. That's better. My body is on fire. Steam bounces off me, taking my breath away. I carry on rubbing the shower gel deep into my skin. I rub until I'm red. Until I'm raw inside and out.

I turn off the dial and look down at my red, raised skin. I have left fingernail marks across my legs. My chest. My arms.

I'm awake now. And the buzzing has quietened just enough to ignore it. The heaviness hasn't gone; the sludge inside still moves as I do. But it's OK. I can manage.

I dry myself hurriedly, and dress just as quickly in my usual trousers and top. I like the protection of my clothes. Once I'm dressed I feel a little more secure. I can relax a little.

I reach for my phone. I post a picture most mornings, we all do – all my mates. I pause for a second, and then I press the camera. Six shots, all bad. One more. I study the image in front of me. I see stupid mousey hair, making my face look washed out. My fringe hangs in my eyes – which are too big, too bulgy. Eyes grey like puddles.

I try again. And again.

I hate every single picture. My face is too long. My hair too wild. I push my hair back. I drop my chin. Look serious. I need to look right. Or at least, I need to look OK.

And the last shot is better. It'll do.

I post it.

Regret floods through me.

"You're wearing *that*? Seriously?" Mum has her coffee cup held in mid-air. She turns her beautiful towards me, unable to hide the disgust that twists her features.

"What's wrong with it?" I cross the kitchen looking for something to eat. As usual I'm not particularly hungry, but it's something to do. And if I don't do it, I'll get a load of questions hurled at me, as if I am about to starve for missing one stupid meal.

"It's going to be at least thirty-two degrees today. You'll boil!" Mum's nose wrinkles at the thought. "You should be out there, soaking up the sun. A little bit of colour would do you good."

I glare back at her. She is seriously the biggest moron I've met; why care about skin cancer just as long as we all look pretty? She used to have her own sunbed until it broke. Now she gets a spray tan from Jessica at the salon. In Mum's eyes it's better to be the shade of a tangerine than, God forbid, naturally pale.

"I'm not going to be lying in the sun," I mutter, tipping out a bowl of cornflakes. I eat them dry; I like them better that way. I hate the way the milk makes them all gloopy and weird. "I'm going to the skatepark."

"Well I expect you'll get hot, skating about." She pushes back her blonde hair, her bracelets dropping down her slender arm. "I mean seriously, Gabi. You should at least wear a short-sleeve top. You could get sick out there, dressed like that."

I keep on crunching my cereal. I wasn't about to change my clothes and she knew it. This is another pointless argument that we keep on having. It's so boring. She'll insist that I should wear a nice sundress and I'll just walk out in my black long-sleeve top and jeans, the same as ever. I don't know why she keeps going on about it. Surely it bores her too?

"I don't want you collapsing from heatstroke, that's all," she mutters. "Aren't I allowed to care?"

I shrug. And just for a minute I think I can see the brief flash of pain in her eyes. Or is it disappointment? Who knows? I've given up trying to guess.

"You don't have to worry about me. I'm fine. You know that. I'm a big girl now."

"But I do worry. I can't help that."

"These clothes are better for skating," I tell her, trying to sound calm and persuasive. "If I fall, the material protects me. That's all. If I wore a dress, I'd tear my skin to shreds."

I see her flinch at the thought. Of course I could also tell her that I feel so ugly and awkward in dresses. That I hate revealing my long, bony limbs. I could tell her that I feel safer, wrapped up in tight, dark material.

But I don't.

How could she ever understand?

"On such a nice day, it seems a waste." Her voice is still soft. She isn't looking at me. She carefully sips her coffee. "We could've done something else. The beach maybe? Something together? I don't know why you have to be there all the time."

There. By saying that, she's just thrown out the grenade. Another accusation that I should be with her instead of with my mates.

I sigh – heavily. Push my hair away from my face. "I'm going to the park, Mum. Like always."

The conversation ends. It always does. She continues to stare at nothing. I continue to crunch my cornflakes. The taste is bland and cloying now.

This is stalemate #78.

The skatepark is five minutes from our house. Two if I run. My journey is a blur. I keep my head dipped down, my body arched. I don't want to see anyone on the way – to have to talk to them, or explain where I'm going. There's a small-town mentality on this estate. Everyone needs to know your business – it does my head in.

The skate-park is right at the back of a scabby, bald stretch of field, where dog walkers and young kids have taken over. You have to watch where you step, because the grass is littered with holes, rough patches and dog crap. There used to be an open-air swimming pool here long ago, before it got all chipped and sharp. For years, it just sat – a great concrete hole, yawning into the sky – before the council realized that kids were freewheeling on it and scratching it up even worse. I guess they decided developing it was a safer option, rather than risk someone slicing their legs open on the rough concrete and suing their arses off.

Building the skate-park was the best thing they ever did round here – and to be fair, they did a decent job. The park itself is a 15-foot-deep wide bowl at the end of a concrete halfpipe with the perfect amount of flat bottom. It also has other banked areas and wooden ramps to jump and progress on. It's always busy, even at night under floodlights. Everyone wants to practise, learn the basics, improve new moves or try out stuff they've seen on YouTube.

It's been part of me for so long now, I can hardly remember a time when I wasn't here. Amira got me into it. I used to keep her company when she first started coming to the park to see Freddie. They'd been mates for ever, and he had a whole gang of skater friends, and Amira liked to sit and cheer them on. But it wasn't long until I was getting bored; I'm not good at sitting around and watching people. I like to be part of stuff. So, I started to borrow boards and have a go – nervously at first, hurting myself, scabs on my knees and hands learning the basics, nothing too showy. It wasn't long before I was hooked. Freddie had found it all amusing to begin with.

"No way," he'd grin. "You won't stick this out!"

I had to plead with Mum to buy me a board. She wasn't pleased; I think she'd have preferred it if I was a track star or swimming champion – something more normal. In the end she reluctantly shoved the cash in my hands and muttered something about it being a "stupid phase" under her breath. But of course Granddad understood. He understood everything.

I'd spend afternoons after school round his, practising on his patio – while he read the paper or listened to music, giving me the odd word of encouragement. He loved it and never criticized, not even when I fell on my arse most of the time. He knew I had to get things just right, knew how much practice mattered. I couldn't do this at the skatepark. I wanted to prove I wasn't a complete dork – it's hard enough being a girl skater as it is. The only other one is Cat, who could be all right if she tried harder – but I wanted to be better than all right. I guess the competitive bug just bit me hard.

And it turned out I *was* good. Really good. Maybe it was all those years Mum spent trying to get me to be a "real girl" at gymnastics, but once I started jumping my balance was spot on. And if I did fall, I wouldn't be put off. I'd just get back on again. It was worth a few scabby knees and bruised up elbows.

Today the park is quiet, with just a few kids I recognize messing around. This is why I love the summer holidays so much – plenty of skating time. I see Freddie straight away. He is pretty hard to miss really – tall and thin with long, messy hair that whips all over the place like a dark cloud.

"Gab!" He waves me over.

He is standing on his board goofing around. All of the guys are with him: Si, who like Freddie is two years older than us at seventeen, but acts like a kid most of the time and is a bit annoying with it; Dylan, who is a year older and OK, quiet and usually wrapped up with Cat; and Alfie, also a year older than me, fairly chilled, but awesome on his board. It isn't until Freddie steps aside that I see Amira is sitting on the grass behind him, listening to music as usual and scribbling in her book. Skating isn't for Amira – she has rubbish balance – but she likes to hang out with us. I guess she likes the vibe. Freddie and her have been dating for a few months now. It's sweet how their friendship naturally evolved into something more. It feels right somehow.

"Hey! We were wondering when you'd show!" he says now. "You're not usually the last one."

"Yeah, well, it took longer to escape today. Mum wanted me to go to the beach, put on a dress. . ." I roll my eyes, making light of it. Freddie seems to get it. He flashes me his lazy smile and returns to the bowl.

My eyes skit over to Amira and I grin.

"How's it coming on?" I ask her, nodding at her notebook where she writes her songs and poems.

Amira sits back, squinting over at me. I'm still getting used to her recently cut pixie crop, which makes her dark eyes look bigger and even more striking than ever. Everything about Amira is slightly sweet and cute, but there's an edge – almost childlike but with an added bite. "Not good," she says, twisting the pen between her fingers. "Nothing's coming right today."

I can see what she's done so far. Lines and lines of

words. Words that were awesome to me, but always rubbish in Amira's eyes. I should say something encouraging, but I feel so tired still, like I am unplugged somehow – barely functioning, blipping in and out of everything. I can't even move closer to her, even though it would be nice to lie beside her, on the warm grass. Not to think or talk at all.

"You OK?" she asks gently. "Did you get my texts?"

"Yeah... I'm sorry. I forgot to reply" I shrug. "I'm just all over the place."

Amira nods. "Don't worry. I get that. I just wanted to check things were OK with your mum?"

"It's OK," I say.

"It's hard for you right now. Don't be too tough on yourself."

I know she understands. If anyone could, she would. Amira always appears like she's got it all sorted, but only the two of us know how much she stresses inside. How anxiety claws at her like a wildcat. I'm the calm one, normally, the confident one. Or I was. Until—

"I got this for you," she says softly, reaching inside her tatty blue rucksack and drawing out a battered hardback book. She hands it to me; the cover is all torn up and has been doodled on in a bright blue pen.

"What is it?"

"An old poetry book of mine. I've marked some of my favourites. I thought you might like to read them." She smiles up at me, her face looking bright and hopeful. "It helped me. Before. When I—" she stops. "Well, you know when. I just found it calming."

"Thanks." I shove it into my own bag. I know she's being kind, but I also know I'm unlikely to even open the book. I'm not someone who does well with words, especially not now. "How are *you* feeling?" I ask her, wanting to change the subject.

She stretches out her legs. "Yeah. I'm OK. I like being here. It's relaxing. Me and Freddie are going out later." She smiles shyly. "It should be fun."

"That's cool," I say gently. "But what about everything else?"

Since her Dad left Amira has struggled big time with things. She's only just started coming back to school.

"It's OK. I have an appointment with a counsellor next week to talk over things. I still..." Amira pauses, her pen scratching the paper. "I still feel nervous about stuff, you know? Still worry about silly things. Still have to do my little rituals to get me through – but it's OK. Freddie helps."

I grin. "You two are so cute!"

She shakes her head softly, but as she turns to watch him, pink slowly tinges her cheeks. Freddie is doing a noseslide, grinding the nose of the board along the edge of the steps. It's an easy trick for him, but the steps are bumpy which makes it slightly more difficult. Not that you'd know. Freddie makes it all look easy.

"He's great isn't he?" Amira says.

I don't need to answer her. He is great. She's great. I feel a sudden wave of envy for what they have. They make it look easy.

"Come on, Gabs, let's try some airs," yells Alfie.

He's standing at the top of the ramp, smiling down at me. He's tall and good-looking, with a scruffy mop of hair. Months ago, he had been like the others and given me stick for trying to join in with them. But now I am accepted. I belong here. Now he is asking me to try some tricks with him.

This is all good.

This is what I do now.

I grin and take my board, stepping up to the ramp. My senses tingle in anticipation. I can do this.

I can't explain it. The feeling as you fly, flip the board and contort yourself in the air. That adrenaline. The burst of life. Just *my* board under *my* feet – just *me* controlling it – nothing else matters at that moment except *me*.

I honestly think these moments are when I feel most alive. When I'm trying to reach the clouds. When the sky is tipping. When absolutely anything could happen.

Only then do I feel properly relaxed. But of course this is the time I totally screw it up.

I know I've taken it wrong almost instantly as I take off – my front foot is too far forward. I kickflip the board awkwardly. On landing my foot pushes the nose into the transition and I go straight over the front of my deck into the concrete.

Hard.

My hand drags against the rough surface, a sickening burning pain rushing through me.

I draw breath, surprised at the feeling. The pain was like a blast of warmth searing through my bones. I sit up carefully, inspecting myself for damage, but the only injury is above my elbow, red and angry.

I see Alfie giving me a look that is part sympathy, part teasing. Freddie strolls over. "Took that a bit heavy, mate?"

"I'm OK." I get up, shrugging it off. Immediately feeling that burst of humiliation. I hate getting it wrong. Hate it so much.

"You seemed ... distracted or something..."

"I'm fine. Really." I stare at him, my eyes drilling

into his. I don't want anyone else telling me how I am feeling, or what I should be doing.

I get enough of that from Mum.

"Fair enough. Going to take it again?"

"Sure."

I flip the board against my leg, catching it on my knee. Of course I'm sure. Right now, there is no place else I want to be.

I'm alone in my room.

I sit with my phone in front of me. I've just taken six selfies. Six. And I look awful in all of them. A complete joke. I delete them all, my thumb scrolling across the screen. Then I sit back. Breathe out and take another shot. My last attempt – it'll have to do.

I watch as my photo uploads. Smiling, carefree, confident Gabi. I already hate it, but I want to be OK again. I want people to see my picture. To like it. To see that I'm still the same person I always was.

Nothing has changed.

To the outside world, I'm still the same Gabi.

I am.

I think back to earlier, to the jump. It's not like me to mess it up. It's because of this weight inside me, maybe. It's shifting now. Like a beast. Icy claws reaching up inside me. No one can see it. No one can understand what it's like to have this. To feel like this.

I just want to go back. I want to make it OK...

I run my fingers back over the red graze on my palm. It burns again. Fire and pain drilling into my bones.

Without thinking, I dig my nail against the skin, sucking in my breath, watching as the blood greets my finger. That burn again, so new. I sit back, pressing my skin all the time.

Red touching white.

Anger greeting numbness.

This is new.

This is a different feeling.

When I was about six, maybe older, Granddad took me to the seaside. It was a bright, cold winter's day so I was wrapped up tight in a huge scarf, gloves and bright blue wellies. I also had a streaming cold and was feeling pretty sorry for myself.

Granddad had decided it would be better for me to spend the day breathing in the sea breeze, rather than sitting in a "stinking pub". Mum had been worried. I think she drilled Granddad a million times, asking where we were going and what we would be doing. I got the feeling she didn't like me being too far away from home. But what other choice was there? Mum was needed in the pub. I wanted to be with Granddad and he wanted a day at the coast.

"Look after her," she'd growled at him, which I thought was unnecessary, but Mum could be a bit like that sometimes. She liked to keep me close. Dad actually stepped in and touched her arm. "It'll be OK," he said, smiling gently at me. "Let her have a day out. She deserves it."

I smiled back at them, wondering why they always

worried like this. Granddad was the best to be with. On the odd occasion he was allowed to have me, he always made things fun and he always brought me back on time. I didn't know why they fussed so much — calling up and checking up on him all the time. Not that Granddad ever minded. He said it proved that they cared. He said it showed they were good parents.

I remember we sucked chewy mints in the car on the way there, the ones Mum never let me have because she said they were bad for my teeth. Granddad played his music loud, his favourites from the seventies — the Jam and the Clash. He sang along loudly and out of tune, trying to teach me the words. His voice was happy. He had a short-sleeved top on and I could see the tattoos on his strong, muscular arms. One was faded blue, but had my mum's name twisted around a dagger that plunged into a heart. Alice.

We parked up and walked along the front. He bought us soggy chips and we sat and watched as the sludge-coloured sea heaved itself against the rocks. I picked up some seaweed and threw it into the water. I remember peering into the grey froth and wondering how anything could actually exist in there, it looked so dirty. Granddad didn't seem to care. He kicked off his trainers and stuck his feet in the shallow part, shrieking like a girl as the cold hit his toes. It made me laugh so much.

We walked back up to the promenade still laughing.

"We used to ride our bikes down here," he said – pointing down the huge road that ran in front of us. "Whole pack of us. God, we thought we were the best things. Mirrors bolted all over our scooters, the more the better. We took over the entire place. I tell you – those were the days."

He breathed in deeply, his thin chest taking in gulps of sea air. "I thought I was king of the world. I believed anything was possible."

He took me to the arcades, pumped money into the flashing machines until more flew out amongst the whooping sounds and flashing lights. We giggled as pennies poured into our plastic buckets. It felt, for a brief moment, like we were millionaires. All the time we were watched by a sour-faced woman slumped at the counter. "Cheer up, love," Granddad said as we walked out. "A smile won't actually break your face, you know!"

We walked across the road. He paused outside an all-day café. It looked worn out and greasy, and the windows were so grimy you could barely see inside. The smell of chips was so thick I could taste it on my tongue. Outside a battered sign stood on the pavement, swinging lopsidedly in the breeze.

"So, it's still here," he said, lighting a cigarette. He went all quiet then and just stood there looking sadly at the creaking sign. I shivered; the excitement of the day had worn off and I was feeling a bit rubbish and coldy again. I wanted to go home.

"I met your nan here," he said finally.

That was the name carved out on his other arm. Rosie.

"One person. One person can really change everything," he said, before moving us away.

CHAPTER THREE

The nightmares are the worst. They claw into the good dreams, ripping them apart. They seem to go on for ever and stay rooted in my brain. I wake up dripping in my own sweat, my duvet across the bed, my hair in my mouth. Everything in the room feels topsy-turvy, and it takes a while for it all to right itself.

In these dreams I'm right back there. At the house. I'm with him.

And every time I can't save him.

I take slow breaths, trying to concentrate on the space around me. I'm no longer in the trap of a dream; I'm here, in my room. I let my eyes drift across, taking in the shapes. I can still see reasonably well because of the thin strip of light around the door and the moonlight outside, which illuminates everything in an eerie glow. It must be the middle of the night. I love my room normally. It is minimal and clean; I hate clutter. All I need is my bed, my wardrobe and my chest of drawers. My only other addition to the room is a black squishy chair that I sink into when I really want to chill.

I focus my eyes on my pictures on the wall, a collection of framed arty shots that Amira took last year. One is of a single tyre swing looking lost and broken, another is of a graffitied bridge across the road from here and the last one is of our ramp, with a skater in mid-air (Freddie, of course). I concentrate on my breathing and fix my gaze on those images; even though I can barely see them in the half light, they are so familiar to me. I feel calmer, but only a bit. I'm still hot and sick, and I go into the bathroom. I plunge my hands in ice-cold water and comb streams of it across my head. I stare into the mirror at my pale, blotchy face. I'm still shaking. Deep breaths don't work. Closing my eyes just brings it all back. I still see the stuff I want to shut away.

How do you stop the bad dreams? The only answer is to stay awake. To lay, glassy eyed, staring at the ceiling and guarding yourself against them. Of course, you can only do that for so long...

Tonight, though, that's what I'll do. I can't face returning to that dark, nasty world. I climb back into bed, my phone in my hand, and try and find something to escape into. Another world, something that stops me thinking.

My dry eyes scan the bright screen.

I'm glad no one sees this.

This part of me.

I look at the last picture I posted, my last selfie. I count the number of likes. The number has dropped since the picture before. Someone has called me "moody and too skinny". Another has commented on my trout lips. I see nicer comments too, but I'm guessing these people feel sorry for me; I almost hate them as much for lying. My heart is racing. I stare at myself on screen, at my stupid, empty face. I do look awful. I always do.

I never get it right.

I must have slept despite myself, because I wake up later to the sound of banging. My phone is on the pillow beside me, I look at the time. It is late. After ten.

I find Mum standing at the bottom of the stairs, the part that leads into the main bar. She has loads of empty cardboard boxes at her feet. Huge ones. I scan them numbly, wondering what the hell is going on.

"Yeah, thanks for the help," she says, catching sight of me and pulling another one down right at her feet. She looks less glamorous than usual today. Her blonde hair is scraped back into a ponytail and she isn't wearing make-up. She tugs at her top, pulling it away from under her armpits. She's sweating a bit and her face is red and shiny.

"I didn't know you needed any." I count at least

five boxes at her feet. *She must be clearing out the loft*, I think idly. "Where's Dad?"

"Your bloody dad is at the bloody supplier again. So I'm on my own as usual."

"I am allowed to sleep, aren't I?" My voice is a little louder than perhaps it should be. "Ten isn't that late."

"Really? I'd say that's half the day wasted!"

"Oh ... Jesus. Whatever!"

I storm into the bathroom to wash, and curse myself for letting her get to me again.

I think of Dad, busy again, like he is most days. He's like a ghost, creeping in when I'm in bed, slipping down to the pub when I'm awake. I know he has to work, but it's still pretty rubbish.

By the time I come out, Mum is back in the main bar, stacking everything by the main doors at the front of the pub.

"Your dad can take these over later," she says, her back still to me. "There are more up there but this will do for now. I can't stand that attic. It's full of dust."

"What are these for anyway? Are you finally having a clear-out of your clothes?"

"Very funny." Mum turns and sees my face; suddenly her voice is a bit softer. "No, I thought you realized. I got these down for Granddad's house. We need to start clearing it out."

Something hits me, I swear, right in my gut; I'm winded. I take a step back, manage to swallow. "What? You're doing *what*?"

"Gabi," she says gently. She comes towards me, like she wants to hug me, but I don't want her near me and I take another step back. "You knew this would happen. It wasn't his house. It's the council's. We have to empty it so that they can. . ."

". . . they can what?"

"Well. Clean it. Rent it out again. People need it. And we need to move on."

I imagine other people in there, in his house. Cleaning, scrubbing. Wiping away his existence. And then later, more people. New people. In his space. Painting his walls. Digging up his patio. Changing everything.

He wouldn't be there any more. Ever. It really would be the end. I can never go there again.

I am no longer cotton wool. I am air. I am drifting.

This can't be real.

"You can't do this!" I yell. "It's still too soon. He's only been dead for a few weeks and we're already packing him away, trying to forget about him."

Her eyes glint, with tears or anger. "Oh, here we go! He was my dad, Gabi. My dad!"

"Yeah, and you act like you're not even bothered," I say, my voice shaking now. "This is easy for you. Throw his stuff away. Stick it in boxes. He'll be gone then. Gone—"

My voice catches. Broken. I'm spinning.

"You think it's easy for me?" she says, her voice small.. "You think it's easy for me to go in there? Go through his things? Could you do that?"

The icy fingers inside me are clawing again, twisting, turning – sending a chill like a breath, an icy whisper into my lungs.

The house. Back at that house.

Those things. Those things you saw. . .

I fight back the sobs. I push it all back again, shove it all back inside.

"You know nothing," she says, her voice brittle and cold.

"You can't do this," I whisper, moving backwards, needing to get away. I can't look at her. I can't stand being with her. She never gets it. She could never understand.

"Gabi." Her voice sounds strained. She reaches out a hand and I see her long nails, red and sharp. I want to snap every one of them. Instead, I pick up the nearest box and hurl it at her. Anything to keep her away. She screams as it strikes her face.

"Why don't you care?" I shout. "What are you going to do? Throw it all down the dump? Pack away every trace of him?"

She is huddled away from me now, shielding her face. Guilt ripples through me.

"You just don't get it, Gabi," she mutters.

"No," I say. "I never do. That's the problem."

*

I am in my room, and the weight inside me is shifting. It's heating up, becoming liquid. It's caressing my throat. I can barely breathe. But I know I won't cry. The tears are trapped, caged.

Without meaning to I pick at my skin, at my graze from the other day at the park. It itches and bites at me. I claw a bit more, my nails sharp and brutal.

I tear easily.

I open myself up; small droplets of red touch the pads of my fingers. It is weirdly soothing. I press harder to make more blood bubble up – a tiny volcano of rage, proof that I actually exist.

Some of *him* is in this blood. I am part of him still, even though he's gone. And I can hurt like he did. The blood fascinates me, the redness of it. It is pure. This thing we share, it is beautiful – untainted and raw.

I look down at the small hole I have made. A small part of me is now *visibly* damaged and broken. It burns and buzzes.

I fall back against my bed. Guilt and a strange kind of pleasure sweep across me. Something...

I can feel something new. A release.

It lasts seconds. Then, the heaviness drifts down and settles like raindrops in my tummy.

After the seaside outing I started to go to Granddad's house more. I had the feeling that Mum wasn't entirely happy about it, but she no longer argued as much. It was as if our outing had been a test that Granddad had somehow passed.

"I want you to prove me wrong. I want this to work," I heard her tell him. "I really do."

Granddad just nodded. "It will. I promise."

At first, she'd insist on coming along. She'd hang around in the background like a drifting shadow, watching, her hands creeping up her arms like she was shivering with cold.

But little by little she relaxed. She'd start to leave me for ten minutes, half an hour or more. She'd let Granddad look after me at his house while she got her hair done or went shopping. Things that she knew I hated doing. She'd ask me if I was OK with it, her face anxious.

And of course I was OK. What a silly question. I loved it there. It was our time. I loved being with him and I loved being with his dog, his lovely sleek greyhound, Weller (named after the greatest singer *ever, he said). On fine days we would take him for walks in the park. We'd throw a ball and laugh as Weller got hopelessly confused. "That dog's got no sense!" Granddad would say, sucking hard on his cigarette.*

On one particular day, Mum really wanted to go to her mate's birthday lunch in the pub but Dad was away. Granddad had offered to look after me "It's fine, you go and have fun," he said. "Gabi can keep me out of trouble."

"Are you sure?" Mum had said, her eyes anxious. "I thought today was your shift—"

"I said so, didn't I?" Granddad was smiling. I saw Mum flinch. I saw her eyes flick towards me, like she wanted to say something else. But she didn't. She just left.

Straight away Granddad cranked up the music. He was all excited about fixing up the car out front and getting a bit of cash from it.

"Exciting things will happen, Gabi. Just you wait and see. If I can sell it, it'll be the start. The start of good things."

The car looked like an old rust bucket to me, falling to bits. But I knew Granddad could work magic. If anyone could, it would be him. "Who needs to work for other people when you can be your own boss?" he muttered, looking far away.

I was fussing Weller, running my hand across his sleek coat. "Don't you like it at the garage?" I asked. I liked it there. It smelled of petrol and paint and was run by a man called Mick who always gave me lollipops. I liked Mick a lot.

"Nah — not any more. Mick and I had a falling out."

"A falling out?" I imagined Granddad tumbling off the roof, hurting himself.

"Mick doesn't want to be friends with me any more, Gabs, but it doesn't matter. That's what life's like sometimes. People move on. But it's OK. I can do things fine on my own!"

He smiled, but the smile looked wrong. It didn't seem to match the rest of his face. I shifted in my seat, wondering why he was looking odd. I wanted to ask him more questions, but something stopped me.

Granddad left the room then and returned with a blue can. I knew it was beer, but it was the first time I'd seen him with one. He opened it and took a sip. "That's better," he sighed.

After two cans he seemed much happier.

"Don't tell your mum," he said, nodding to the empty cans. "She'll only worry."

I nodded, and climbed on to his knee.

"I have something for you, Granddad," I said.

I'd been holding it tightly in my hand – it had got a little creased but it was still OK. It was just a picture. Silly really. Just the two of us holding hands. I'd carefully crayoned Granddad's black hair and smiley face and carefully drawn in my own blonde pigtails. Around us was a lopsided pink heart.

Granddad stared at it for a long moment, then he gave me a quick hug. "That's beautiful," he whispered. "The best thing ever."

And he slipped in his wallet. Where it stayed.

CHAPTER
FOUR

I'm in Amira's room and I'm telling her all about losing it with my mum. She looks at me; all the words are there inside the deep, dark depths of her eyes. Her mouth curls into a semi-smile. She shifts off the bed and joins me on the floor.

"Oh, Gabi, it's OK. Come on," she says, rubbing my leg. "Don't beat yourself up over it."

"I threw a box at her. Even she doesn't deserve that." I pick at the threads of Amira's rug, twisting a strand around my fingers, pulling hard so that the top of my finger turns white.

"So..." she sighs, settling herself down next to me. "You argue. It's bound to happen. You've had it rough lately. You just need to take your mind of things for a bit. Focus on other stuff – like the skating! Freddie is so impressed with your skills right now. And Alfie. He spent ages the other night going on about how good you are."

I feel my cheeks redden. "Really? I'm not that good. I still keep decking. My balance is shot."

"Gabs, you're seriously good. You need to get a look at yourself." Amira made a funny snorting noise. "Honestly, when you're at the park, everyone is looking at you. Not only are you annoyingly good looking, but you're crazily talented too. That's not fair."

"Don't be daft." I could feel myself getting frustrated.

"I wish you'd believe me—"

"I don't believe you when you talk crap." I flash her a warning look and then break it with a wary smile. "Look, I know you're just trying to make me feel better, but I don't need to be told that I'm 'good looking' or 'talented' or any rubbish like that. . ."

"You know I don't lie about this stuff." She frowns. "I wish I had your balls!"

"My balls?" I giggle. "I hope I haven't got those." I look up at her, at her serious face. "Amira, you don't need to be anything like me. You're fine as you are. You're like the academic queen – you're bound to be a superstar businesswoman and rule the world or something."

She's still frowning – it's tiny, but it's there. As kids she used to sit right up next to me, take my hand and ask me over and over, "Do you think it'll be all right? Do you think it'll be OK today?." She'd always find something to worry about and whatever it was, I'd have the answer.

That was then.

"Is everything OK with you?" I ask her gently.

"I guess," she sighs. "It's just with Dad gone ... most nights Mum is working late and I'm here alone, checking the locks ten times over. It's crazy. Now I've got it into my head that..." she pauses, shakes her head. "Silly stuff again."

"What is it? Tell me?" I say.

"It's like ... do you remember how I used to worry about something bad happening, all the time? Now it's kind of worse. I panic that something might happen to Mum. That she might get hurt or, or something..." she finishes softly, her expression lost.

"That won't happen."

"I'm so scared of ending up alone. I know it's stupid, but my head just won't shut up. The thoughts, you know? They won't stop."

"You'll never be alone!" I say, but all the time I'm thinking, *I know that feeling! Those thoughts that won't shut up. The bad feelings. The sick crawling in my stomach.* I go to open my mouth. I go to tell her. But then she speaks again.

"I just wish I was like you. You're so together. Even after everything that's happened to you, you just get on with it. That makes me feel inspired, like I can do it too, you know?"

I nod weakly. "I know."

Because I do know she needs me. She needs me to be the strong one. She always has.

"I hate being this pathetic," she mutters. "I can't even tell Mum; she's got enough on her plate."

"You're not pathetic. And if you're scared at night, just call me," I say.

"Really?" she smiles.

"Of course." I nudge her and grin. "I'm pretty nice aren't I?"

"Alfie certainly seems to think so." Her voice is soft, almost teasing.

"What?"

"Well – according to Freddie, Alfie really likes you." She looks at me cautiously, gauging my reaction. "Has done for a while, apparently."

I dip my head and continue to pull at a thread in the rug. I'm not sure what to make of this. Alfie is lovely – a little quiet maybe, but really nice. Good-looking. Funny – a laugh, but smart. I can't believe for one second that he'd be interested in me. He's had girlfriends before, really nice ones. Dead pretty ones. Ones who were clearly going to college. Girlfriends like Amira. Not gobby freaks like me.

"He's going out with Freya, isn't he?" I ask.

"Not any more. They split up months ago. Freddie told me that Alfie has been going on about you for ages, but he finds you..." she pauses. I look up and see that she is staring right at me. "He finds you a bit, well ... scary."

"Scary?" I almost laugh in her face. "How the hell am I scary?"

"Well, you do have this 'front'. I like to think of it as your protection; it's what makes you 'you'. You don't like people getting too close to you. Just in case."

"In case what?"

"Well ... in case they hurt you."

"That's rubbish!"

I sit back. The thread is still pulled around my finger. I tug at it again, feeling the pinch of the skin.

"I'm just saying..." Amira's voice is softer now, and she gently touches my leg. "I'm just saying that you find it hard to let people in. To let people know the real you."

I keep staring at her dark eyes. They are so warm. So calm. She's always been able to see the real me.

I can feel something stir inside me, the buzzing again. The uncomfortable, squirmy thoughts. I blink.

"That's not true," I say. "I let people in."

But we both know I'm lying.

I churn over these thoughts as I sit between Mum and Dad at dinner, trying to eat. Amira's right. I shut people out. There's only two people who have ever really known me. One of them is Amira and the other one is no longer here.

No longer here. . .

Dad is rushing his dinner, as usual. Actually it's a miracle he's there at all. The pub is due to open in half an hour. This is how life is for us most days – living for the pub. Watching the clock, living our days by opening and closing times. Living by the bell. It's always been my life, but it doesn't stop me resenting it. I can't remember a time where we've done something different. Broken with routine. Gone out for the day, together. It's been even worse lately. At least there were more staff before. Nowadays it seems like Dad is holding the place together on his own.

Mum is very quiet. I notice she has a tiny red mark above her right eye. If you didn't know it was there you wouldn't see it. But I see her put her hand up to touch it, and she winces. That has to be an act. Surely it can't hurt her that much?

"Are you going to talk about what happened earlier?" Dad says finally. He shoves his plate aside. Gravy spills on to the tablecloth and I notice Mum flinch.

"Earlier? I went to Amira's." I push the meat around the plate. It is thick and fatty. I hide it under the mash.

"Before that," he says, a little louder. He is trying to sound firm, but I know he's distracted. In front of us the clock is ticking. There is lots to do. He wants to get on. He can't stand sorting out domestics.

"We had a row. Mum was winding me up." I flash her a look, but can't help seeing the red mark. "It's over now. Can we just leave it?"

"You hurt her, didn't you?"

"It was an accident. I was angry."

"It wasn't *an accident*." Mum speaks, and she really hisses the words. I wonder if she actually hates me now.

"It was. I threw the box. I didn't mean to hit your face." I state each fact clearly in bullet point fashion, like she's the child. "I'm sorry if I hurt you."

The apology is lame; I know this and so does she. She stares at me with her hard eyes. Her lips are parting and I wonder if she wants to say more, but instead she grabs her glass and takes a long sip.

"Thank you," Dad says instead. "See, Alice, she is sorry."

He gets up quickly, humming under his breath. In his eyes it's all sorted and he can go back to business. He knocks the table again and more gravy spills. I see Mum's grip on her glass tighten. The gravy darkens the material, a deep mud-like stain. We are both looking at it, knowing how much it bothers her.

I turn to my own dinner. To the cooling carrots and grey-looking peas. I've only had a few mouthfuls but I already feel full. I use my fork to push it all to one side, letting the soppy potato drip on to the table like a dirty volcano. I can feel her despair clawing into me, but she says nothing. She's obviously not in the mood to make a fuss. I hear her take another drink. Then she sighs heavily.

I pick up my dripping fork and knife and dump them on the table, old food now congealing on my side.

"Thanks for the dinner, Mum," I say sweetly.

And I walk out, leaving her to clean up my mess.

Later.

I sit on the edge of the bath. The door is locked. Downstairs the pub is in full swing. I think I can hear the muffled voices of Mum and

Dad rise and fall. Mum's is louder of course. She is laughing now. Now that I'm not there. It's a melodic, happy sound. My sounds are dark and ugly. They don't belong in this house. I just bring everybody down.

For a brief minute or so, I rest my head against the wall. I can feel the soft thump of the blood in my head pumping rhythmically. I count the beats softly, trying to channel out the other stuff. Trying hard to focus.

I feel dizzy, probably because I had the hottest shower ever. I felt like I needed it. It made my skin buzz and burn. I stepped out of the cubicle shiny red and tingling all over, feeling sick and giddy from the heat. But feeling ... something that wasn't dread, unease, panic.

But now they are rising again: flutters of terror, tiny fingers of ice squeezing my stomach, caressing my chest. I am buckling with the sensation. I want to drive a fist in my belly. I imagine all the bad stuff shooting out of me – bursting out of me like a water fountain. This can't carry on, surely? I am bloating up with bad stuff. Heavy with it. I can't get it out. I can't.

I don't remember reaching for the razor, but suddenly it's in my hands. It's a pink plastic one – an old one of mine. I hold it for a bit. Stroking the long bend of the plastic, reaching up to the tip and running my finger across the blade – not too hard at first. I can feel the roughness of the steel, its bite. I press it first against the tip of my thumb. Then, without really thinking too much about it, I press the blade out from its protective arm. I free it. The metal is in my hand, small and shiny. And sharp.

I breathe out hard, still a little giddy. I shake my head. I know the dark thoughts won't go. The buzzing. I need to feel in control again.

I breathe again. Harder. And then I bring the blade down across my arm, allowing its sharp tongue to greet me.

Sweeping. Pressing. Cutting. Pain tugging my skin. But not really pain, something different – something deeper. All the time I can hear the laughter from downstairs, ringing through my head, hurting my ears.

All the time I am trying to pull out the darkness from inside me, tug it out from me like a leech sucking out poison.

The blood flows out and I feel it again. The release. Something dark coming out from deep inside of me. My breaths are slower now. I'm calmer. I can stop.

As I sit, staring at the bloody rivers on my arm, the shame hits me. Sickening and gut wrenching. It makes me want to hammer the floor with my fists. Makes me want to wail into the steam-filled room. Makes me hate everything that I now am. Ashamed and helpless.

I place my head once more against the cool tiles, clutching my arm and watching the blood thicken and clot. I haven't let the bad stuff out. It's still there. Inside me.

Mum used to have a name for me, growing up –
Little Miss Angry. I didn't like it much, but it didn't
stop her using it.

One time, I heard her talking about me in the
kitchen. She thought I was playing, but I wasn't. I
was hiding behind the door. Of course it was Aunt
Gloria she was talking to – always Gloria. Gloria
had always been a part of our lives, but it was
only around this time that I worked out she was
Granddad's sister – not that she looked anything
like him. Where he was thin and dark, she was
curvy and blonde. Granddad called her the "good
one" of the two. He said she was the one who made
the "right decisions", whereas he was the "mess up
of the family".

I didn't understand that at all – he seemed fine
to me – but I did understand that the two of them
weren't close. In fact, I never saw them together.

Gloria seemed to practically live at our house,
sipping tea in the kitchen and eating all the nice
biscuits, whilst she filled the air with her sweet
perfume. Usually I was allowed to stay in the room

as she and Mum talked. But this time Mum asked me to leave. She said she had a headache and needed some quiet time with her auntie.

But I didn't go. I knew Mum was upset about something. Her eyes were all red and small, and even Dad's hugs weren't helping. Something bad was bothering her. So instead, I hovered outside of the door like a trapped shadow, catching the snippets of conversation.

"She never listens to me. I don't seem to have any authority over her at all. She screams, shouts, slams doors. It's like I'm raising a monster!" Mum was talking, and her voice was hard and brittle like a drill hammering into my head. "I never expected it to be like this. If I'd known..."

"I'm sure it's just a phase..." Gloria's voice was soothing, trying to make it all better.

"It's my fault, I guess. Everyone told me I was too young – that I wouldn't know what to do. I wouldn't listen..."

"You're a great mum!"

"I'm not. I'm not a natural at all. And Jack's

always working in the pub so he can't help much. There's only one person who has any effect on her now. Why on earth does it have to be him?"

Him? My ears pricked. I held my breath. My heart was thumping so hard I thought it would burst clean out of me.

"He's her granddad, Alice. It's good that he has some involvement in her life."

Granddad! I gripped the door edge with my tiny hands. Why was mum so angry?

"She loves him so much. And that's a good thing. But..." Mum was saying, sounding so sad now. "I just don't see why she can listen to him and not me." Her voice sounded strange, wobbly. "And why him, of all people? There's no one who'll understand, once you're gone..."

"Alice, I'm not going far – Manchester! I'll be on the end of the phone!"

"I know. I know."

I stepped back, shocked. I didn't know Gloria was moving – no one had told me. I knew this would be hard for Mum.

Another noise. Was that sniffing? I wasn't sure — I moved my face up closer.

". . . I just can't bear to think of . . ."

There was a clattering of china. I couldn't hear properly. I tried to press my ear against the door and lost my balance. It swung forward, revealing me and my bright red cheeks. They both looked up and saw me.

"Gabi!" Mum gasped. Then she turned to Gloria, her finger pointing. "You see. Always sneaking around, listening in on stuff. She's just like him. That's why they get on! As thick as thieves, the pair of them. I can't trust him. And now I can't trust her either. . ."

CHAPTER
FIVE

"Amira! Your hair is amazing" Who cut it?" Mum is gushing, like she's part of the gang or something. It's embarrassing. But Amira just smiles.

"I went to Zero's. Do you like it?" Her fingers comb through the front nervously. "I'm still getting used to it. My neck feels so cold all the time."

Mum giggles. "Oh, it won't take long! I went short about your age. I keep telling Gabs that she should do something different with her hair, but she never listens!" Mum turns to me, hands on hips. "I mean, I know you're lucky to be natural blonde, sweetheart, but your skin is so pale. It doesn't help that you *refuse* to wear bronzer or blush. Why don't you think about highlights? You know Gilly would do an amazing job!"

"No thanks," I mutter.

There's no way in this existence I'm ever going to let Mum's mate Gilly near my hair. She will peroxide it in a blink, and knowing my luck, it will all fall out. Then I'd be bald *and* pale. A lanky alien skating through the park.

"Gabs's hair is wicked as it is," Amira says loyally. This is why I totally love my mate.

Mum's nose wrinkles a bit. "I suppose. So what are you girls up to today?"

Again. I don't know why she feels the need to ask this question. Our plans are always pretty much the same day to day.

"We'll chill here for a bit and then go down the park," I say.

"We'll get Freddie on the way," Amira adds.

Mum nods. "How's it going then, at the, um, park? Learning any new tricks?"

I'm actually cringing inside for her. I just wish the pub was busier, or she had a date with one of her orange mates so that she wasn't hanging around the flat with us, asking lame questions and trying to act cool.

"Well, I'm still rubbish," Amira says, "but Gabs is getting so good. She's as good as any of them. Yesterday she totally rocked an air jump, and that is sooo difficult to pull off."

Mum is looking totally blank. She doesn't say anything for a bit, but then she smiles. It is small, almost nervous. "Sounds ... cool."

"It's totally cool," says Amira

It's totally not *cool,* I think, staring at Mum.

She turns and smiles at me. Our eyes lock for a second and then we both look away.

"It's so lame! Why does she have to hang around like that?" I kick at a can in front of me.

I'm in a rubbish mood now. I really wanted a chilled morning. A chance to relax and chat with my mate. Instead Mum had to poke her nose in.

"Ah. I think she just likes to make sure you're OK. Find out what you're up to. It's sweet."

"It's not sweet. It's interfering, irritating and bloody annoying. Your mum's not like that."

"No, I guess not," Amira says. "But then she's hardly around."

Amira's mum is awesome. She works her arse off as a nurse, and now has to work even longer shifts since Amira's dad left them last year.

"Yeah, well, your mum's not the type to stress if her fingernail breaks, is she?"

Amira laughs. "Your mum is so cool, honestly, everyone in our year thinks that. I mean, you could borrow her clothes and make-up – how great is that?"

"Yeah ... great."

"Seriously. You are really lucky. She's dead sweet."

I bite my lip, feeling a bit bad. She is beautiful, my mum. I can picture Dad in my head, his arm wrapped around Mum's waist, his face burning with pride. He won't have a bad word said against her. She is like a queen to him.

We are passing the small parade of local shops. The shop fronts are pretty grim; most days there is a window smashed in or a bin set alight. An old "phone card" sign is swinging above Del's shop, slightly lower than it should be, probably because some other nutter had already dragged it down. Everything round here is bashed about and falling apart.

"Look. I bet I can grab that sign!"

I don't know what's got into me, but I want to change the subject from Mum. Before Amira can say anything, I drop my board and leap up, feet flying. I hoist myself up and my hands quickly grasp the overhanging metal pole that juts above Del's. It is rusty and rough, but I manage to hang on, swinging like a monkey and laughing, my legs dangling freely.

Amira is staring up at me, frowning.

"All right, all right! I'll get down!" I say, shaking my head at her disapproving look.

But then I see where her eyes are resting. They are not on my face. They are on my arm. My sleeve has ridden down and she was staring right at my ugly red scar.

I drop quickly, landing neatly on my feet. Amira is still looking at me, her face creased in concern. Just across from us, some younger kids are terrorizing a small dog that is tied up to the fence. Its yapping is starting to hurt my head.

"Let's go," I say, keeping my voice light.

"How did you do that?" she says, reaching out a hand to my arm. "It looks nasty."

"What?" I try to act dumb, picking up my board and trying to ignore her burning gaze.

"Your arm, Gabi."

"Oh, that – it's nothing. I did it on a jump."

She is really staring now. We've known each other since we were little. She knows when I lie. She always knows.

"You need to clean it up properly," she says finally. "Something like that could easily get infected."

I pull my sleeve back down, feeling the burn as the material grazes the exposed skin. The dog is still barking.

Shut up.

Shut up.

*

Freddie lives just across from the park, in a small terraced house. It's pretty grim looking, grey with tiny windows and a shabby door with yellowing sellotape criss-crossing the glass. In the garden, three deflated footballs sit in the long grass. I don't think Freddie's ever even played football. They must've been there for years, just lying there – all forgotten.

Freddie literally tumbles out of his door, followed by Si, Cat, Alfie and Dylan. They hang around the house most of the time, if they aren't at the park. I don't think Freddie's mum minds. In fact, I don't think she's around very much to care either way.

As usual, Freddie sweeps Amira up in a huge hug. He is double the size of her, so he can pick her up so easily. She giggles and beats her fists on his back. "You crazy lump. Put me down!"

"I can't help it! I'm just excited to see you! I thought you'd never get here." He spins her around until she squeals.

Amira pulls away from him, stroking his long

hair affectionately. Cat stands behind, hands on her hips, shaking her head. "You guys are too cute."

"We're cute too," Dylan says hopefully. That is probably stretching it a bit. Cat is super-cool – I often look at her bright red (dyed) hair and striking eye make-up and wonder if I should go for a change. And Dylan has a shaved head and several facial piercings, and he's tall and muscular. *Cute* is not a word I'd use to describe .

Freddie runs over to me in two easy strides and kisses me on the cheek. "Gabs, you are looking as gorgeous as ever."

"What is up with you?" I say. "Did your mum give you three Weetabix for breakfast or something?"

"What's up with me?" His eyes are sparkling. "I tell you what's up with me. It's a wonderful day. We're about to skate our arses off, and I've got fantastic news. Haven't I, Alf?"

Alfie is standing just behind him, shaking his head slowly and smiling. He pushes his dark hair away from his eyes. "The guy's a nutter. . ." he says to me. We both grin. I feel suddenly shy.

"Not a nutter!" Freddie goes back inside, shoving past Si and Dylan. He returns clutching his board tightly. "C'mon, you lot. Si, just pull the door shut behind you. Not too hard though – the bloody glass might shatter. Let's get going while the sun's out. We never know how long we've got! I might even tell you my big news on the way."

"Freddie!" Amira is fake-whining and walking next to him. "What's going on? You have to tell me. I have rights!"

Alfie draws close to me. "He's on such a wind-up today," he whispers. "He'll probably keep this going all day just to annoy Amira."

"She'll end up getting it out of him!" I say. "She might be small, but she's fierce, believe me."

"I can believe it."

We trot down the hill towards the park. Behind us Si, Cat and Dylan are discussing moves. Ahead Amira is thumping Freddie and laughing. Alfie and I have fallen into step together.

"So how are you... I mean, after everything," Alfie says softly. He shifts his board under his arm. I can tell he feels awkward. "I hope you don't mind me asking. I keep meaning to."

"I'm OK, thanks," I say. "I mean, it's been horrible and everything. But I'm OK."

We keep walking for a bit. No words. Then Alfie says:

"Well – if you ever want to. I dunno... I just wanted to say, I'm here ... if you need anything."

I glance over. Alfie's cheeks are a soft pink, and his eyes have dipped towards the floor. It's a shame he always hides them – they're a lovely greeny-brown. It's a bit naff, but they remind me of the colour of autumn leaves. You can't always see them, because his hair tends to fall over them, like a dark shade.

"That's really kind of you," I say. "But I'm OK. Really."

"Cool." He nods.

I rub my arm as I walk. I can still feel the burning, and the heavy ache inside. But it's better when I'm with this lot. If I concentrate hard I don't notice the feelings underneath.

Not as much anyway.

Freddie makes us wait all afternoon before he makes his announcement. We're stretched out flat in the sun, exhausted from skating. Amira is playing tunes on her iPod. Everyone is feeling relaxed and cool – except for Cat, who is texting. Her and Dylan had been arguing all afternoon and now they're sitting apart. This is pretty common. The pair of them break up once a week, only to get back together the following day.

"I'm going to have a party," Freddie declares. "It's going to be immense."

We all look at him. Cat stops texting. Amira turns down her music.

"Your Mum's OK with that?" Amira asks. She looks worried.

"Yeah, sure. She's always at Ryan's now so she's not bothered."

Dylan smacks the grass. "Result!"

"Nice one!" Si is on his feet, punching Freddie on his arm.

"It's going to be wicked. Si – you can get some tunes playing. We can wake up the whole neighbourhood!" Freddie is now lying on the grass, a small smile creeping on his face. "This summer everyone will be talking about Freddie Lawson's party! I will be a legend."

"So, you want us to get the word around?" Alfie asks.

"Yeah. Of course. Next Saturday. The more the better. They can smash the place up as far as I'm concerned. I'll doubt she'll even notice."

I look at his face and notice a flash of something pass across his eyes: a hurt. I moan about Mum and Dad being on my case all the time, but it must be hard living with people who don't even notice you. But then Si throws himself on his stomach, ruffling Freddie's hair. "Fred! This is awesome. We'll smash the place to the ground."

"This could be a disaster," Amira whispers to me. I see her eyes are wide and round. She's thinking ahead already, worrying about all the options, everything that could go wrong. And Amira's not really one for parties, but I'm guessing Freddie doesn't know that.

I look away and Alfie catches my eye. He smiles a slow, happy smile.

"I'm looking forward to it," he says.

All the time his eyes remain on me.

Granddad's house was just around the corner from school, closer than home was – five streets away. I guess you could just about call it a house, but it was tiny – so squashed up against its neighbours, it looked like it was breathing in. Granddad called it a "two up, two down", which basically meant there was room enough for him, the dog and his collection of junk.

The house itself was tatty and tired looking; the white painted walls were all chipped and the windows were pretty grimy. The front door was a faded red with a small window criss-crossed with metal squares. I liked to trace my finger across them, feeling the small bumps under the glass. It backed on to a big, graffiti-covered warehouse, and the house always seemed to be in its shadow. But Granddad liked it. He called it his "humble abode".

There was no front garden really – just a battered driveway where Granddad kept his bikes and the car he was fixing. A few flowerpots stood randomly against the splintered fence, filled with dried-up soil and cigarette butts that were withered like fingers curling up towards the sky. Weeds grew in every direction, winding and stretching across the broken slabs of concrete and wooden slats. The back garden was small and full of junk. Old car parts littered the yellowing grass. I wasn't really allowed out there in case I hurt myself on the rusty machinery.

Instead I stayed out the front. On good days, I would sit on the broken doorstep watching as Granddad worked on his car or tinkered with the bikes. He'd have his tools spread out all across the concrete and usually some music blasting from a small radio plugged in via a trailing lead from the kitchen window.

He'd bang and hammer away whilst whistling and singing and telling me the odd joke. Sometimes I'd sit with a big block of chalk, drawing circles and funny faces on the ground. Other times, I would read a book or a comic, quite happy in my own little world – just as long as I was part of his too.

We'd sing songs together. Granddad taught me the words of his favourites. We'd sing loud and out of tune and every so often he would hit the paving slabs with his tools, like he was playing the drums. He always looked the same: crazy hair, red cheeks and a huge beaming smile. He seemed so tall, so strong, so full of life.

But some days Granddad wasn't so up for fixing things. Or playing music. His face looked different somehow, sullen and grey. His body seemed to lose shape too and he became lost in his own clothes.

On those days, we would sit indoors and Granddad would be slumped in the armchair with his legs spread out wide. He'd drink from his special green cans and put a yellowing finger to his thin lips. "Don't tell your mum," he'd whisper. "She'd only fret. Promise?" And I'd nod. He'd let me eat all the biscuits and drink all the Coke. My teeth would feel furry and my tummy a bit swirly. I'd lay on the sofa with Weller, watching him rubbing his face with his big, rough hands.

Then he'd fall asleep on his chair, mouth open, spit curdling in his mouth. I'd creep out, careful to shut the door behind me.

I never told Mum of course. I'd made a promise.

CHAPTER SIX

I am sitting in the bathroom. One scar, my very first, is just starting to fade now. It looks less angry, a slightly softer red, as the mark is re-absorbed back into me. I press my nail against it, watching as it changes colour again. I don't like to think that it will disappear completely; that feels wrong somehow. The marks are part of me. I can't forget this. It's not something I can let go of. I imagine my scar running deeper inside me, marking my muscles, to my blood vessels and bone. Every time I press it, I can feel the electric shock vibrate right down to my core. It catches my breath. It reminds me of everything I am inside.

Downstairs, far beneath me, I can hear the

heavy rumble of chatter and laughter from the pub. It's always there of course, except during the depths of night, and even then I still think I can hear it. The pub seems to carry the sounds all the time, a constant echo chamber. And Mum and Dad are always there – holding the fort, running the place, looking good.

If I tip my head slightly, I can just about hear the deep tone of Dad's voice drifting up. Then more laughter. He is so popular, so well loved. They both are. Everyone says so. "Jack and Alice – what a great couple!" Round here they are like some kind of king and queen. Does that make me the princess? I smile bleakly at the thought.

From deep inside me that twisted pain is building again. It always creeps up so slowly, like a sensation of hunger or fear. It's gnawing at my stomach, pulling at my chest. I want to move my whole body against it, ram my face against the wall and scream to make it go away.

What is wrong, Gabi? Why can't you move on? A persistent little voice rings in my ears.

I blink away tears. Why *can't* I move on? This is stupid. I can't keep being angry with my parents. I can't keep feeling sad about Granddad. I am such a screw-up. I should be able to pull myself together. Everyone else seems able to cope with way worse stuff than me. I shouldn't be doing this. It's wrong. I'm a mess. But I can't stop.

Why? Why the hell can't you?

The inner voice is taunting me. I hate it. I dig a fingernail deep into my scar, flinching at the biting pain. Yes, of course I deserve this. All of this.

I want him back. He understood me. He got me. No one else does...

I'm alone.

I've hidden the blade behind the mirror. Having it in my hands again is good; it feels natural. The cool metal feels right between my fingers. Like it belongs there.

Alone.

Now I'm slicing fresh skin, high up on my thigh. Hidden skin. The burning, twisting pain is sickening. I am dizzy and my hand is shaking. I have to really concentrate, to take time over what I am doing, but the voice inside is quieter now, even if it hasn't totally gone away.

Alone...

Alone...

Blood trickles. I pat at it gently. My torn flesh stings, weeping red.

Still, the churning inside is calmer now.

For how long? the little voice whispers.

I make a rough bandage out of padded tissues, and pull some pyjamas on over the top. The bleeding is pretty bad this time – worse than I'd expected. It's hurting to walk a bit too. I curse myself; I don't want this to affect my skating.

I'm lying on the sofa in the living room when I hear the last punters leave and Dad lock up. Mum comes upstairs first. She always does. She clatters into the living room and kicks her shoes off, so that they fall upside down in the middle of the room.

"Oh. You're still up?" she says, her mouth forming a perfect "O" shape.

"Obviously." I sit up from the sofa, throwing the magazine I was reading to one side. "I wasn't that tired."

"Well, I guess there's no school," she replies. "I remember when I was your age. I spent all the summer holiday at some party or another. Great times!"

I nod. "That reminds me. Freddie is having a party next weekend. It's OK if I go?"

"Freddie?" Mum looks vague.

Dad walks in, rubbing his face. He looks exhausted. "What's this about a party?"

"Which one is Freddie again? Is he the one with the funny hair?" asks Mum, attempting to mime mad hair with her hands.

"Yes. He's dating Amira. He's been here before – you kept going on about how tall he was!" I cringe again just remembering it.

"Oh yes. I remember now." Mum nods enthusiastically. "Nice lad."

"This party. There's going to be boys there too?" says Dad.

"Well, dur! A boy is hosting it! It'd be a little weird if he only invited girls."

"No need to be sarcastic. I just like you to be careful."

"I will be, Dad."

Like you care...

It's the mean little voice again. *Of course he cares,* I think.

"I think it's great." Mum is beaming. "You can get a new outfit. I can get you a spray tan if you like? Do your make-up for you?"

"No, it's OK."

I see her face fall a little, and I feel bad. "I just like doing it myself, Mum. Maybe you could straighten my hair though?"

"Could do." She walks over and strokes my head. "But your hair is lovely, Gabi. You've always had such beautiful long hair. So thick. But we can make it look really glossy!"

"You girls!" Dad shakes his head. "I'm done in.

I've got to hit the sack." He flashes a final look at me. "You can go to this party. But no drinking. And I'm picking you up."

"Yes, no drinking!" Mum echoes, her face hardening. The one thing Mum is super-strict about is alcohol. It's kind of ironic that she works in a pub and never touches the stuff. I guess she's seen her fair share of drunks at closing time.

"It's OK – Amira's mum will get us," I tell Dad.

He pauses, then nods. "OK then, just as long as she does."

I watch as he walks away. The tiredness is so obvious – it seems to cling to his body, changing his entire shape. But this was his life. I've never known my dad to not be completely knackered by the end of the night. I wonder if he actually enjoys it as much as he makes out.

"Oh my god, Gabs! What have you done to yourself now?"

Mum is sitting right up and pointing at my leg. Panicked, I look down and see that blood is seeping through the material of my pyjamas. I jump up and the pain bites.

"It's nothing – I grazed it earlier."

"But it's so high up!" Mum looks confused.

"It's nothing. I'm fine."

"Can I at least check it?" She reaches towards me.

"No, please."

"I'm your mum. Let me see!"

The anger bursts out again. Quicker this time – like fresh lava from the pit of my belly.

"Just leave it, Mum! Just leave me alone! Stop interfering!"

"Don't talk to me like that!" Her face is flushed now. "I have a right to know what's going on!"

"Oh, so it's OK for *you* to ask questions?"

"What's that supposed to mean?" she hisses at me, body bent forward like she's about to launch herself.

"I dunno..." I shake my head. I'm tired. Everything is hurting and my head is starting to throb. I pick up my glass of water and start to leave. "I'm going to bed now."

"No! No, you're not! What do you mean, it's OK for me to ask questions?" She is standing up now, hands on hips, trying to look all in control and angry, but I can see her arms are shaking.

"I mean – you never let me ask any! You never want to talk about him. He's been dead over a month and we still don't talk about him. About what happened to him, how he got so bad. I know you two had problems, but you won't tell me about it. I feel like I only know bits of stuff. I feel like you're keeping things from me."

There. I've said it. I risk a look at Mum and see that she's just staring at me.

"Don't you care?" I say. "Don't you even care that he's dead?"

"Of course I care," she whispers.

"You don't though," I hiss. I can't help it. "I know you two had problems. I bet you wished he'd never come back."

"That's not true, Gabi!"

"It is. You hated him when he was alive. You hated me being around him!"

"I just wasn't sure his house was always a . . . suitable place for a child." Mum is flailing. "And you spent more time there than here some days."

"Did you blame me?" I say. "Dad's never around anyway and you—"

"I'm what?" Her voice is cool.

"You're just not interested," I say. It's rubbish and not fair, I know that, but I've said it now. I drop my head and blood rushes to my cheeks. I feel sick.

"I can't believe you could say that." I hate it when she sounds so sad.

"I'm sorry," I mutter. "But I just don't get it. I don't get why you close up about Granddad. I feel like I can't talk to you about stuff."

Like what happened. That day.

Because how can I open up to you, if you won't to me?

But she's not really listening. She's got that lost, far-off expression. She's not even looking at me now.

"I just. . ." She pauses and then lifts her head

a little. "It's complicated, with me and your granddad. And I don't have to explain this to you but I just ... I don't want to talk about him now."

"You hated him!" The words snap out of me. "And you hate me, because we're so alike."

"Gabi!" I can see the shock on her face. I know she wants to say something more, but I'm out of there.

I'm done listening.

I can't sleep. Lying in the semi darkness, I try to focus on the single beam of light coming in from the hallway, where I'd left the light on. Who apart from Granddad had known that I was still terrified of the dark? I hate the sensation of being swamped in blackness, of nothingness suffocating me in its huge, ugly weight.

I like brightness. I like light, breaking things up, allowing me to see everything, even at night. Nothing unexpected can get me. Nothing nasty can be waiting in the shadows. Bad things always seem to happen at night, in the shadows or when you aren't looking. Monsters lurk in the dark.

It's a fear I can't seem to lose.

When I was really little I had nightmares. Bad ones – vivid twisted dreams. I'd cry out in the dark, begging for someone to come and save me. At home, Mum would have the TV turned up loud, and Dad would be in the bar. No one came.

But Granddad understood. He got it. He stroked my head when I told him about the monsters, about the devilish looking creature that hid under the bed. He told me to draw pictures of the beasts and then to tear them up into small pieces. Together we threw the shreds into his fire.

"They won't get you now, Gabs. We've burnt them away. You're in control. I won't let anything bad happen to you."

I turn on my bed, flinching slightly as the cover brushes my leg.

"Everyone else is asleep," I whisper into the sheet. Talking to him. Am I crazy? Maybe. *"Why doesn't Mum ever talk about you? It's like you were never*

here at all. What did you do? Why weren't you ever close?"

I reach for my phone, my eyes blinking hard at the sudden glare. I want to see who's online now. If anyone is free to talk. Sometimes Amira is up late, if she is busy writing or caught up in a film. Freddie is always online. And Cat. I see Alfie's profile, flashing green. I click on it.

I love his picture. He is facing away from the camera and smiling at something off in the distance, probably one of us. His hair is typically scruffy, falling across his face in dark strips. I flick through some more of his pictures. There is one of him and a small white dog. Another where he is standing smiling with three people who I assume are his mum, dad and younger brother. My God, he looks so much like his dad – they have the same eyes! His family life looks nice, normal. There are dog-walking pictures, birthday parties, lots of photos of Alfie skating, and in every one he looks so gorgeous and natural. You can also kind of tell that he's a nice guy – I'm not sure how. There's just something about him, a kind of vibe that's difficult to describe. I'm typing before I can think:

Hey

I wait. Only seconds and then he types back.

Hey. You OK?

I am scrolling through more of his pictures. There aren't many, he's obviously quite selective. But I notice there's one he's uploaded a few months ago – of all of us, a massive selfie. We are sitting on the bottom of the ramp. I remember it being taken – I was shouting at Si to hurry up because my legs were cramping. Our faces all look so huge and mine is pressed right up against Alfie's. I keep staring at that, wondering why that's making me feel so weird. I see he's typed again. *You're up late. What's up?*

My fingers hover over the screen. There is so much I want to say, but where do I start? And who wants to hear depressing stuff anyway? Who really wants to hear what I am thinking and doing?

I suddenly remember Fliss Rogers. She was

someone who used to come skating quite regularly last year, until she got a bit intense. Freddie and that started to call her an emo and a loser because she cut her arms pretty bad. She didn't even bother to hide the scars – it was like she was proud of it or something. Fliss stopped coming to the park eventually; she could tell we had no time for her. The group would laugh at her behind her back. And I'd been as much a part of it as anyone.

Alfie wouldn't like this part of me. No one would.

I'm OK, I type. *Looking forward to getting on the board again.*

He replies quickly. *How about tomorrow morning? We could get there early. Get loads of practice in.*

Sounds good. See you then.

I close the app, trying to force myself to feel happy. This is good. I will meet Alfie, I'll have fun, he'll take my mind off stuff. Skating helps me; it always has.

I skim through the Internet for a bit, and

without really stopping to think why – with Fliss Rogers in my mind still, probably – I type in the words "self harm" into Google.

Loads of sites come up. Lots of advice stuff that I just flick past; I'm not ready to read all that. But there are forums too. One is called Hidden Scars.

I have to register first, which is easy enough. Within seconds I am Ska8erGirl15. I scroll through the posts; there is so much stuff on there. So many people sharing their stories. Some have even posted images. I flinch as I click on one picture, lines and lines of red, jagged raw skin and the words underneath: *I was really mad today*. The post has loads of replies, mostly messages of support, pleas to get help.

I log out quickly, feeling suddenly shaky and a bit confused. I don't know how I feel about this. I wonder if Fliss goes on sites like this. She's not someone I know well. She doesn't even go to my school. My head is so jumbled.

Why do I even care? I'm different anyway. I'm not like them.

I'm hurting for different reasons. I won't even do it again.

I'm different.

I imagine Granddad here. Somewhere with me, close by. Shaking his head. Smiling. Telling me not to worry. *"It'll be OK, Gabi. It will. You'll stop missing me soon. These feelings will go."*

And: *"It wasn't your fault. What happened that day."*

But could that be true? Really?

The strip of light dances in front of me and I close my eyes against it. I imagine everything is just as it used to be, imagine nothing has changed.

I imagine I'm not this person any more.

We were lying flat on our tummies, the grass brushing against our faces. It had been a long, hot afternoon. One of those summer days that seem to go on for ever. I was feeling so sleepy, drunk on sunlight, and my eyes felt heavy as I watched the skaters move back and forth across the ramp. They were gliding, their wheels making a rhythmic thud against the cement, lulling me further into a daydream.

One day soon that would be me...

Amira was writing, her large curvy script covering yet another page, her tiny face screwed up in concentration. She paused and scribbled a section out, then sighed, throwing the pen aside.

"I'm not in the mood today," she said.

"Don't stress. Try again later!"

Amira looked at me and half smiled. Telling Amira not to stress was like telling the sun not to rise.

I reached for my gum and handed her my last one. She took it, popping the tiny white square between her teeth.

"They were fighting again last night," she said finally. "I'm guessing this time might be the last.

Dad slammed out, said some awful things. Mum has been crying again. I hate it there. I hate it all."

"I'm sorry," I stroked her arm. "Maybe ... maybe, if they hate each other that much, then it's for the best though?"

"Maybe." She shrugged. "It's silly, isn't it? I can't stand it when he's there. And I hate it when he's gone. When it's just us alone I get even more scared. I think of all the stuff – all the bad things that could happen to us. I worry even more."

"Nothing bad will happen," I said gently.

"But I hate thinking of it just being us two. Only us. It makes me feel scared," she whispered.

"You're not alone. You have me too!"

Amira turned to me. I could see the sparkle of tears in her eyes. She took my hand, all big and clumsy in her dainty one. "I wish I was strong like you," she said.

"Don't be silly," I giggled, squeezing her.

"You're made of steel, deep down," she giggled back.

"Just talk to me. Whenever. I'll always help," I

said. "I'll always be there."

Amira smiled at me, a soft, lazy smile now. "Thank you," she said. "You don't know what that means to me."

But I did. She was my best friend. I'd do anything for her.

CHAPTER SEVEN

Minutes after I wake, I open the Hidden Scars website again. I can't help myself. It's like my brain never really turned off in sleep. It was the first thing I thought of on waking.

As if to convince me, my thigh, now stiff with dry blood, stings as I sit up. A reminder of what I've done to myself, of what a mess-up I'm becoming. So before I can let self-doubt trickle into my cluttered brain, I make my first post as Ska8erGirl15.

Thread: Hi

Hi guys. My first post on here. I think I might

need to talk. I never thought this would be me, if you get what I mean. I just never thought I'd need to post on something like this, but I'm just not sure where else to go.

If I'm honest, I've always felt crappy inside, like I wasn't quite right, like I was a bit of a disappointment to my mum. I never let on. I was always the confident, gobby one. But then recently my granddad died. We were dead close. There is so much stuff I feel bad about and there's no one I can really talk to about it. My friends are cool, but I don't like to bring them down.

The first time I hurt myself it was just with my nails, but it seemed to help. It was just good to get all that pain out. But now I'm starting to cut. And I hate myself afterwards.

So here I am, just saying hi and hoping that you'll understand. I need someone to.

I finish the post and press send before I can change my mind. Then I shut down my phone and sit for a while in the stillness in my room.

Sometimes I feel like there is nothing of the old me left; just a shaky mess.

"That was awesome, Alfie – seriously awesome!"

Alfie comes back over, cheeks flushed. He's been leaping over the steps leading down to the park. A series of proper neat ollies. It's a pretty fundamental trick where you and your deck leap in the air as you skate. I just love watching him – he takes each short flight with such ease. I know he's been good at them for ages, but it never fails to impress me how clean he takes them. He's just so natural with the board.

"Why, thank you!" His eyes twinkle. "It's only taken me, what, two years to master?"

"You are so good though. You could do this professionally like Ross and his lot!" I say, feeling the excitement build. And what was this? Maybe a touch of jealousy. Yeah, I'm good, but I'm not even close to Alfie's standards.

"Nah, Ross lives and breathes it. I'm happy just doing this for me."

"Well, I still think you're as good."

Ross Finch is eighteen and pretty much the king of the board. We all want to be him. There was a time when he owned this park, but now he is at so many events we barely see him.

"That's why I like coming up here early. It's so quiet – I can really concentrate. I swear I do my best jumps at this time." He turns to me. "I'm glad you came too. I hope you're not too tired though. You were up pretty late last night. . ."

"No later than you! And you seem to be coping."

He shrugs. "I don't sleep much. My head's always buzzing, I can't switch off, you know?"

I nod. I know.

"It's nice you're here though. I can never get the others out so early."

I laugh as I remember Amira's sleepy voice when I called her earlier. *"You're joking! I'm not getting up for at least another hour!"*

"They do like lazy mornings," I say.

Alfie sighs. "It's so true. Freddie never digs himself out until gone midday – that's half the day gone. It's such a waste."

I smile. "You sound like my mum."

"Seriously, just look up at the sky. It's pure summer. It's beautiful. The mornings are the best, fresh and clean. The air tastes great. It gives you more energy," he laughs. "Jesus. I sound like a crazy hippy!"

I tip my head back. Swirls of blue and white move above me. The sky does seem bigger and brighter. I imagine mastering all those clean ollies that Alfie has, being able to jump as high as he can. It must feel like touching the clouds, being part of the light and ripples of marshmallow sky.

"You don't sound like a hippy at all," I say.

"Good." He moves a little closer to me. I notice how long his eyelashes are, how a tiny dimple ripples in his cheek as he smiles. He's dead cute, there's no denying that. He looks even cuter this morning somehow – it's like I can really see his energy, his beautiful waves of sunlight. He is so happy and radiant. It's infectious.

"I wanna do some kickflips," he says. "Join me?"

I hesitate. Kickflips are harder than ollies. I'm pretty poor at them. It's when you spin the board 360 in mid-air during a jump. It can be hard to pull off – I often end up decking.

But this is why we're here, right? To make the most of the time? I also have a burning desire to leap into that beautiful sky. I want to breathe those clouds deep into my lungs. And I want to do it in the most awesome way possible.

His hand touches my arm. "You can do it, Gabs. Just remember where to put your feet on the board, position them right – similar to the ollie, but with the leading foot towards the edge – and then use your toes."

I move forward to the ramp, the pain still there, burning in my thigh – twisting and biting whenever I try to do something too fast. I push the pain to the back of my mind. I don't care. It isn't important. Right now the only thing I want to do is to get this right.

I shift forward, knowing he is willing me on.

I turn. One quick glance back at his face, that

lovely cute face that now stirs the bottom of my tummy.

He smiles. Then nods.

I take a deep breath and turn back around. I swear I can still feel the warmth of his sweet smile against my back.

I jump.

Afterwards, we sit on the bench at the base of the ramp, giggling like loons.

"See, you're amazing too!" Alfie says, rubbing my back. "You seemed to just hang in the sky for ever. And that landing – man, you nailed it! It was better than mine, honestly."

"Well, thanks!" I say, smiling. "It's so addictive! I just want to take it again!"

"I know. I always feel like that."

It's still so quiet here. There is no one else, just us two. I can hear a distant rumble of cars from the main road behind us, a man shouting at his dog from across the field. But apart from that, nothing. I actually feel myself begin to relax.

I stretch out my legs, enjoying the space, loving the calm feeling inside of me.

"I'm doing an early start again," I decide. "This is so cool."

"You should. It's totally worth it."

The bench is long but Alfie is sitting so close that I can feel his warmth seeping through to me. It is weird, but a nice weird. I reach for my hair, wild and free as usual, and tuck it behind my ears. I suddenly wish I'd put make-up on – made myself look a little more special.

Why am I even thinking this?

"Freddie's party should be a laugh," he says. "We're going to get a huge sound system over there. Invite most of the school – well, most of my year and Freddie's anyway. It should be great."

That meant pretty much most of Year Eleven would be going and most of lower sixth if Freddie, Cat and Dylan were sorting out the invites. That's cool. Most of my year are either dull or annoying.

"I can't wait," I say, and it's true, I love a party, a chance to hang out with my mates and see cool people – but for the first time ever I'm worried about what to wear. Most of my wardrobe consists of black jeans and tops.

"You OK?" Alfie asks.

"You keep asking me that lately," I say, grinning broadly to show there's nothing wrong. "I'm just stressing about girl's stuff. What I'm going to wear. Nothing interesting."

"You'd look awesome in whatever," he says softly, and a hint of a blush rises in his cheek. "Oh, shit. That sounded so naff – but you know what I meant."

"It wasn't naff. Thank you."

Even though it wasn't true. I look awful in most things...

There's a bit of a silence between us. But then I feel the question rise inside me, the one I've been meaning to ask.

"Alfie, do you remember Fliss?"

"Fliss?" He looks blank for a minute. "Oh, that girl who used to hang around here with Ross? The one that couldn't stand up on a board?" He shakes his head, unimpressed.

"Yeah – that one. Do you know what happened to her?"

"She doesn't go to our school, does she? No clue. Can't say I miss her much."

"Alfie!"

Alfie shrugs. "Well, she was a bit of a nut, wasn't she? Always going on about her problems."

I hesitate. "Didn't she used to ... cut herself?"

I keep remembering her arms now, how she used to swing them around freely as she tried to balance on her board. The scars had run all the way up them – like faded bracelets.

"I hope she's all right," I say.

"I don't know why you're suddenly worried. She hasn't been around here for ages. Freddie knows her, I think."

"I know. I just thought about her the other day."

"I wouldn't worry. Most people just cut for the drama, they like to get attention. She lapped it up. She wasn't getting much here, so she probably found another group to annoy." He stands up.

"Come on. This is depressing. Let's go back up there and have some fun."

I dip my head, wanting to close my ears against this. My hand is gently touching my leg, stroking the outside of the wound. Part of me wants to scream at him, wants to say, "I'm doing it too." But what would he think of me then?

He'd think I was another Fliss. Another nut. Another attention seeker. Another loser.

He'd want me to annoy someone else...

I take my hand away and keep my mouth firmly shut. Instead I follow towards the ramp, but I no longer feel like I'm flying. That horrible, heavy feeling is back.

My wings have gone. I'm sinking again.

www.hiddenscars.com

Thread: Re: Re: Hi

You guys are so cool. Thank you for the advice and being so nice about everything. I feel less of a freak about it all.

It makes no sense, but now I've hurt my leg – I keep poking at it and making it worse. It's got pretty bad so I had to put a bandage on. Even then I keep pressing on it. I like the feeling. It burns and stings, but I keep pressing it. Holding it down. It feels like some pressure is coming out, some bad stuff.

I'm going crazy, aren't I?

I reread the post a few times, before sending it off into cyberspace. I imagine the other people that might be reading it. Invisible faces, but with scars like mine. Something shifts inside me. I hate it that I connect with people like this, but it's also one of the most positive things I have found lately.

Beside my leg, my phone buzzes gently. It's Amira. I shut down my laptop, almost paranoid that she can see. So stupid. I couldn't tell her about this. She'd be so upset. I don't want her having to worry about me.

"Hi!" she says straight away. "How was the skate? I'm so sorry I missed it. Did Freddie show?"

I smile. "Nah, he wasn't there either. I swear you two have some kind of psychic connection."

"What do you mean?"

"You know. If you don't come, he doesn't. Without even trying, you two have become a proper couple."

Amira groans. "Don't say that. You know we're not like that – joined at the hip, one of those soppy couples..."

I laugh. "Before long you're be declaring your undying love for each other!"

She squeals, almost bursting my eardrum. "No way! That won't happen!"

"I think it's sweet."

"Yuck, no, not our style." I can hear her moving around. It sounds like she's walking. "So anyway, how did it go this morning?"

"It was cool."

"Who went?"

"Just me and Alfie."

There was a pause. Then: "Really?" I could hear her grin through the phone.

"*Really.* It was cool. Chilled."

"I'm sure Alfie enjoyed it," Amira says, meaningfully.

"Amira. He's not interested in me, not that way. I'm just a skating buddy."

"He so is."

"I can promise you he isn't." *Or he certainly wouldn't be if he knew the true me...*

"You shouldn't be so dismissive."

"Seriously, Ami, I think you've just got this all wrong." I pause. "Do you mind not going on about it?"

"Sure..." She sounds taken aback. "You OK?"

"Of course," I keep my voice light. "We've got loads to look forward to – like the party."

"Yeah," she agrees, her voice is quieter. "Like the party."

"Have you talked to Freddie about it yet? Told him that you get anxious in big crowds, that sort of thing?"

A pause. "It's so silly, Gabs. It's just a party, isn't it? It's meant to be fun. But I just think of all those people, the noise and the madness. It's not my kind of thing really. Freddie knows I worry, but I don't want to bother him about this. He's so excited. He wants me there. I'll have to go, for him. I've just got to learn to chill."

"He would understand."

"I know. I will talk to him."

"Everything will be just fine, you'll see," I say.

I'm strong. I'm there for my friend.

But all the time I'm thinking of the words I've just typed and sent off into the void.

I'm not going crazy.

Am I?

I should've been sitting there doing my homework, but I was now eleven and the skating bug had well and truly taken hold – all I wanted to do was be outside. My board was a part of me. I was lost without it.

The pub was in a half-lit gloom. A few regulars sat watching a snooker game on the TV in the corner. A woman at the bar chatted on her phone. It was still early, about five-ish. Mum and Dad were the only ones working. Dad had his arm draped loosely around her shoulders. His other hand reached across her face to tuck a loose strand of hair away behind her ear. She giggled softly and stroked his back in return.

I sat back in my seat and watched them. My parents. So in love, so protective of each other. I couldn't imagine one without the other. A sudden warmth swept through my body. Then I looked down at my maths homework and a feeling of dread returned. I wanted Amira there with me. She'd help. She'd knock out the equations in seconds and I could be free to have fun outside. But Amira wasn't here. She was spending time with her dad. She was probably as miserable as me.

I must have been daydreaming still when the doors crashed open. The sudden gust of cold air made us all turn towards the source. I heard my dad curse, which he rarely did in public. My stomach twisted and I instinctively turned away from the noise.

Granddad walked in. I say walked, but it was more like an ugly, shameful stagger. His arms were extended wide and his legs seemed too heavy and awkward for his body. Even from metres away I could smell him – I could smell the stench of drink.

"Granddad..." I said, as he walked past me, but it was as if he couldn't see. He only had one sight in mind.

"Alice!" he said. His voice was loud and distorted. "My beautiful Alice. I'd like a whisky please." He walked to the bar and slammed coins down in front of my mum. I watched as they rolled across the wood. He swore loudly.

Mum seemed to be shrinking into Dad, who stepped forward a little.

"Billy. I'm not sure I can serve you," he said. "Haven't you had enough already?"

Granddad froze. I saw his cheeks redden, the muscles in his neck work harder. "Don't be like that, Jack. I just want one drink. Just one more. One drink with my family to celebrate a win on the horses."

"You need to go home," Mum said, her voice barely a whisper.

"But I won today. A good win. We can celebrate together – all of us!" His voice was a whine now.

"I don't want to celebrate." Mum's voice didn't sound like hers. It was cold, far away. "I want you to go. You're drunk, and ... and you stink!"

"You need to shut your mouth!" Granddad said loudly. "That's always been your problem—"

"You need to leave now!" Dad shouted.

The woman at the bar had ended her call. I saw how she eyed Granddad nervously, how she drank her drink quickly and left without a backwards glance. The guys around the TV looked over curiously.

Granddad didn't leave, though. Not at first. He turned slowly, a weird smile fixed on his face. His eyes finally found mine. At first, it was as if he couldn't focus, couldn't quite see who I was. But then his grin grew wider. It seemed distorted somehow – not like his at all.

"Gabi! Gabi. Do you hear what they are saying! Do you see how they treat me?"

He stood, trying to move towards me clumsily, knocking a stool flying.

"Gabi! Come here!"

The coldness crept across me. There was part of me that wanted him gone. That hated having him there, showing us up like this. Making everyone look at us and judge us.

But another part of me couldn't stop looking at his eyes – at his huge, confused eyes, trapped in that red swollen face. I knew he didn't want this. I knew he couldn't help this.

He was still my granddad.

This wasn't what he wanted.

"Please go home, Granddad, please!"

He looked stunned for a moment, as if he was uncertain about what to do. He stumbled a little, turned, and as he did his foot became trapped under the fallen stool behind him.

His fall was heavy and slow. He fell with a sickening thud against a table and then landed in a groaning heap on the floor.

I was the first to him. Mum was next. And she was sobbing.

"Dad ... Dad ... when will this end?"

CHAPTER EIGHT

I knew that agreeing to go shopping with Mum would be a bad idea, but I had no idea *how* bad. As we march into the sixth shop, my head is already pounding and I'm longing to be somewhere else. Anywhere else. But Mum has that determined look in her eye. There's no stopping her.

"There will be something in here," she says, her eyes sweeping the shop. "I just know it."

"Mum, I've had enough," I say, but I might as well be talking to the shop dummy.

"Please," she says, looking at me, her eyes glinting. "I just want to have one nice day together with the two of us. One day where we're not arguing? Please?"

I see something in her face, almost like she's pleading with me to make this work, so I nod. "OK, OK."

Mum grabs the nearest sales assistant, a tiny girl with bright red hair and a smile that seems to reveal all the teeth in her mouth. Her eyes are small and cold though, and cannot hide her obvious dislike of either us or her life in general. She gives us such a fake beaming welcome that I immediately want to flee in protest.

"I'm looking for something for my daughter," Mum points at me, even though we're the only customers here. "She's going to a party."

I feel like I'm about five years old and going to my first McDonalds kids' party.

"I liked that top earlier. It was fine," I say. "Can't we just go back?"

I liked the first shop. I always go there. The top was just what I needed and would go with my jeans, plus it didn't cost much so I wouldn't feel indebted to Mum for a million years. And anyway, it was Freddie's place I was going to – not some prom (thank God) or posh event (double thank God).

"It was black," Mum hisses at me. She turns to the sales assistant. "She has to stop wearing black. It's so limiting. She's so pretty, but she never shows it. Her entire wardrobe is black, black, black."

The girl nods. She is still fake smiling. "We have some fab animal-print dresses at the back," she says, gesturing.

I am cringing. This is just not me. I don't wear print. I barely wear dresses. I pull away from Mum and move over to some rails behind me. I figure if I'm stuck in this place, I might as well take control of it. Mum is off, plucking things from rails and crowing in delight like, "Oh, this would look amazing!" and, "If only I were ten years younger," and giggling. She loves playing the age card because she knows she looks young and can get away with most stuff. To be fair she is younger than most of my friends' mums, but that's only because she decided to get pregnant at seventeen.

I try and busy myself looking at the clothes, but there's nothing I like. It's not my style in here. Mum walks over, holding up one of the print dresses. It's bright blue. I can feel my muscles stiffen.

"This colour would look great on you," she says.

"I'm not wearing a dress."

Mum sighs, holding it against herself. "I'd love this."

"You buy it then. You've got better legs than me anyway."

Which is true. My thighs are heavy and thick. Mum's are long and lean. I guess I take after Dad in all the wrong ways.

"That's not true," she says, but I think she likes the compliment. "Just try it on. For me."

"If I try it on, will you leave me alone?"

"Of course."

Sighing, I snatch the stupid dress out of her hand and stride over to the changing room at the back of the shop. The shop assistant trails after me.

"You need to take these in," she says, handing me two other items and a bright orange plastic disc. I swear she's having a laugh. She's given me a bright pink fluffy jumper and a denim mini-skirt. I glare at her.

"I'll wait outside," says Mum, helpfully, placing herself right outside my chosen cubicle. She'd probably come in with me if she could. I pull the purple curtain against her grinning face and turn. There are three mirrors, one facing me, and two on either side turned at an angle. I guess this is so you can see every side of your outfit, or body.

Neither is good.

"Are you ready yet?" Mum's voice is excited.

I scramble out of my clothes quickly and pull the dress on. It fits but feels scratchy against my skin. I look in the mirror, at this bright, loud material plastered against my pale skin. I look stupid. Like a big joke. The bottom of dress skims my thighs, showing off their hefty, muscly shape.

I hate it.

And then, as I step back, I realize just how

short the dress is. My red scar is peeking out, looking even more nasty and angry than ever. The rough material catches it as I move. I have to get this off.

"Gabi! Come on!" Mum is restless.

"Wait," I mutter.

I reach up to pull the bloody thing off, just as Mum whips the curtain back.

We sit in the car in silence for most of the way. In the bag between my legs is the black top. The one I liked first. The one we should've just got straight away.

Mum hasn't put the music on so I know she wants to talk. She's just finding the right moment. This is so desperately awkward. The silence is killing me – it's draining. I feel like she's sucking all of my energy just by being in this car, by sighing loudly and crunching the gears in that clumsy way. This is all deliberate. I don't know what she wants from me. A full-blown confession? A weeping admittance that I feel rubbish and cutting myself seems to help? What if she asks me why? Even I don't understand that.

She leaves it until we're five minutes away from home before she speaks. Her voice sounds loud now and cracks slightly.

"Don't tell me you hurt your leg skating, Gabi. It looks too ... I dunno, too clean."

"Well I did. Am I a liar now?"

"Those were clean lines. Like cuts. I'm not stupid."

Before, on a really bad day, I would've thrown that back at her. I would've listed all the times she *had* been stupid, all the evidence I'd stored up. But this is not the right time. I just feel tired. I turn away from her, stare out of the window at the numerous houses we pass, each with a neat, tidy front garden. Each with a locked front door and curtained windows, hidden secrets locked away – everyone has them.

"You shouldn't have burst in on me like that," I mutter.

"You were taking ages. I thought you had finished."

"Well ... I wasn't."

Mum's hands are gripping the steering wheel tight. "We need to put cream on it. It looks sore."

"OK. Fine."

"Are you sure there's nothing you want to tell me?"

"Mum. Please. Just leave it."

We pull into our road. The pub is there on the corner, the sign "The Crown" is swinging slightly in the breeze. I used to love the picture of the grand old king, smiling out on the street. I used to imagine that he was related to us in some way and that those jewels were hidden in the pub somewhere for us to find. Now he just looks useless and fat like a pompous old fool, and the picture is all worn and tired. It needs replacing, like most of the stuff inside. The pub itself is dark and sprawling, dark brick and concrete garden. There is nothing bright or pretty about it – although Mum tries with her overflowing flower baskets and ornate benches. People come here to get drunk and forget their problems; they do not come here because it's a nice place.

"Promise me you'll stop," she says quietly.

She's looking right at me now. This is the first time she's done this since we left the shop. She's really staring at me. All I can see is the disappointment reflected in her eyes. Her daughter, the constant mess-up. How did everything go so wrong?

"Just leave it, Mum," I say.

"Promise me," she says again. Firmer now. "Gabi. *It has to stop.*"

"Whatever."

I shake off her stare and open the car door, clutching the bag and that stupid top in my hands. I never wanted to go on this shopping trip. None of this was my idea. I never wanted her interference – ever.

"Gabi..." she says, but her words are lost as I slam the door. The sound is satisfying. I turn towards the grey, faceless pub frontage and march away from the car. A crisp packet swirls under my feet and I stamp on it.

I don't know how long she stays in the car, but she doesn't follow me in.

I go into my room.

Later I do put antiseptic cream on the wound, like she asked. It is sore, so I rub it in hard. The cream was waiting for me on the bathroom shelf. There didn't need to be a note or anything, Mum's instructions were clear enough.

Clean it up. Sort yourself out. Make all of this go away.

It is my fault that it hurts so much still; it is my punishment. I'm glad it is so red, so angry. It is a reminder of everything I deserve. I rub the cream so hard that it stings. And then I rub harder still so that it starts to go numb again.

It's a cycle I'm getting used to.

Mum has pretty much ignored me since we got back. She has spent a lot of time in her room, which is unlike her. Dad went in there for a bit, but then he went back to look after the pub. He's not said a word to me, which makes me think she hasn't told him about my leg. This surprises me. I thought it would've been the first thing she'd do. She must be so disgusted with me that she can't find the words.

Maybe she actually really hates me now. I wouldn't blame her.

I still feel angry about the whole thing. The changing room, the situation in the car, her accusing stare, the old feelings bubbling inside me. As I rub my skin, I pinch and pick at it.

Again, the swirling increases. I can picture the tears inside me, rising and falling, as if they are becoming a tide. A sweeping sea in my stomach, churning and twisting – and then amongst the waves those icy claws rise again, sending sparks of ice down my arms, my legs – all through me. I can't stand it.

Please, just stop this. Stop this now.

Breathe. Try to breathe.

But I can't breathe. The tears are rising up, choking me again. I will be sick. I will gag on my own breath.

It's like the autopilot kicks in. Another me. The grieving me. I need the release. I have to let this out.

I choose a higher spot this time, on my other leg, and I'm slower, much slower. The pain is deeper and more intense – I suck air hard, shaking as the razor drags into my flesh. Blood bubbles and trickles against the white of my skin. I follow it with my finger.

I dab and stroke.

And then I cry, silently as usual. Watching as the tears mingle with my blood.

What a total screw-up I've become.

I still kept going to see him. I had to after that visit to the pub. Who else was going to keep an eye on him? Not Mum, that's for sure. She just seemed angrier than ever. Called him a drunk and a loser. Said she had no time left for him.

So who else was there?

Things were shifting, changing too fast. It was as if a light had gone out in Granddad and I couldn't find a way to turn it back on.

The next time I saw him, he had a nasty cut on the side of his face and his nose was a funny shape. He'd flinch every now and then, running a finger across it.

"I'll be fine," he'd say, but his eyes were far away.

"How did you do this?" I asked.

"I fell, that's all. . ."

Things were different in his house too. He'd pulled a tarpaulin over the car outside, said he couldn't face working on it now. His bikes were gone and so were his tools.

"Where?" I asked.

"It doesn't matter," he said, but he looked sad. Really sad.

He didn't want to walk Weller either, said he was too tired. Said his back hurt. So I took the dog out instead. We went over to the park, had a runaround. I wasn't gone for long though. I didn't like to leave him. I needed to make sure he was OK. I knew that Mum wasn't happy about me going round any more, but someone had to. Someone had to look after him.

I would go round after school and make him a cup of tea. I talked to him. I told him about school. About Amira. About the pub. I'd talk until my throat was dry.

He'd listen and he was always interested. He'd tell me that my visits "brightened up his day" and that I was his "little sunshine".

He didn't drink the tea though. He'd let it go cold. He'd drink from his cans instead. Sometimes he'd fall asleep in front of the TV and I'd put a blanket over him to keep him warm.

I figured that once his bruises healed he'd be better.

But his bruises faded and nothing really changed.

So, I told myself that it was his back that was the problem and once that was better, he'd be OK. He'd work on his car again. He'd go on dog walks. We'd laugh again.

But a year passed and Granddad just seemed to become more and more lost.

I just became more determined to get him back.

CHAPTER
NINE

www.hiddenscars.com

Thread: Re: Re: Re: Hi

It's getting worse. I can't seem to stop. I know some of you have suggested going for a walk and stuff or listening to music, but that doesn't help me. Not right now.

I'm a bad person. This is why. No one else would get that. A bad daughter. A bad granddaughter. I screw up everything.

I'm just here to say ... I don't know really...

I just don't want to do this any more.

Skating is a real problem today. For one thing, both my legs are killing me, so it's impossible to move properly. Plus I've barely slept. It's like I'm lugging a dead weight around.

I choose to flop next to Amira and watch the others, feeling frustrated at how good they're all getting. Alfie is becoming awesome. He moves so effortlessly, like a bird. He looks particularly good today in his low-slung jeans and black top. He's getting a tan and he's had a haircut. It's still fairly long at the front, but you can see his eyes better. It really suits him.

"I can tell you like him. You've been staring at him for ages now." Amira was lying on her front, but now pulls herself up and shuffles closer beside me. "You might as well just admit it."

"Alfie – nah. He's just a mate." I look away and concentrate on Freddie instead, who's messing about on the side of the ramp.

"Why don't you join them? You must be itching to get out there."

"I've got a stomach ache. Maybe later."

"Ah … OK."

"Anyway it's nice sitting with you for a bit. What've you been writing?"

Amira laughs. "It's rubbish."

"I bet it's not."

"It is, honestly. I'm just sketching out ideas for a play. A kind of friendship thing. You know, about loyalties and gangs and stuff."

"It sounds cool." I smile. "I would offer to read it but I know…"

"… that I would never let you." Amira grins. "No offence, but you know my rules. No one reads my stuff until I finish it. I'm just paranoid like that."

"No, it's OK – I get it… I would love to, when you're ready though."

Amira nods. "I will let you. I promise. Hey, maybe you should try it?"

"What?" I shift again, cringing as my leg brushes the grass.

"Writing. It can get lots of emotion out. You've been through loads, with your granddad and that…"

I shake my head. "Nah. It's OK. I'm dealing with it."

Amira sighs. It's such a soft sound, but it irritates me.

"What?" I snap.

"Nothing... I just..." Her voice drops out of range totally. She pushes what little hair she has now out of her eyes and stares up at me. It's hard not to be drawn in by her warm, deep gaze. "I'm really worried about you."

"Why? I'm fine!"

Bang. Bang. Bang. I can feel my defences snap up immediately. If I was any more of a coward, I would've said something nasty to her by now.

"But ..." Her cheeks go very pink. And then she's talking all in a rush. "Gabs ... you're ... you're cutting, aren't you?"

"No!" I spit the word. My cheeks are flaming. "No! I'm not!"

"But I saw your arm the other day – and your mum..."

Oh right. Here we go.

I should have guessed.

"My mum what?" My words are so icy it scares even me.

Amira just blinks, says nothing.

"My mum WHAT?" I stand up now, pick up my board. I'm shaking.

"She's just worried about you." Amira's voice is small – she's not used to standing up to me – but steady. "She wants to help."

"She wants to butt out." I start to walk away. "And so do you."

I leave the park, still shaking. My leg throbs and my heart beats so hard I think it might burst out of me.

I walk away from the park, moving across the back of the field and looping off across the railway track. I don't want to go home so I head towards town instead. I can't face another row with Mum. It's so pointless and exhausting arguing with people that never listen. I can feel my phone buzzing inside my jeans pocket, but ignore it for now. Instead I make my way towards the level crossing. The signal is already wailing and the huge barriers slowly make their way down. As a kid these things used to terrify me, especially the piercing whiny noise they make. Even now, I have stand a few feet back, not wanting to be too close to the gleaming tracks, worried that the clanking barriers would make me jump, make me fall forward. . .

I remember walking in town with Granddad, clutching his huge, strong hand and feeling so safe. We used to make bets on which direction the train was going. If he won, I had to feed the dog when we got back. If I won, I got a lollipop. My whole body used to fizz with excitement as I willed the train to come in the way I'd predicted.

Even now, standing here, I was playing the game.

It's going towards London, Granddad. It's going west. . .

A hiss and creak of the tracks first, and then

the gush and whoosh of the train itself, throwing grit and dry air into my face. I blink hard and taste the bitterness. I watch as the train moves away into the distance, gone in a heartbeat.

I was right. I won. Where's my lollipop?

The gates rise suddenly with a jerky rattle, and once again I jump slightly. Then I find myself moving automatically, down the high street and into the main swarms of the town square. It's busy for a midweek day. I guess the sunshine draws everyone out. The cafés are full outside, as people sit and relax in the sunshine. Across from me is the shop where I'd been with Mum. The one where she saw my scars. I see a sales assistant, a different one, in the window adjusting a shop dummy. Behind her a girl my age is peering through the racks. She looks so cool and relaxed, like she belongs in a place like that. Unlike me.

I walk away and sit on a wall at the corner of the square. There used to be a water fountain here, but it's been broken for months. Now it's just a big useless metal ball. I feel in my pocket.

I find a hairgrip in there. It's perfect. I fish it out and gently ease it between my fingers, untwisting the metal. Then I quickly drag across the skin of my arm. A short, sharp cut, enough to make me take breath. Enough to empty me of these negative thoughts – my brief release.

A busker plays in the corner, strumming a guitar – old stuff that I vaguely recognize. I find the words are tumbling on to my lips, the melody is moving me, drawing me to another place. Of course, this is stuff Granddad used to play. More memories. I feel the sickness lurch inside me, but I can't stop listening. This was his music. I used to love listening to it. As much as it hurts, it's comforting too.

I close my eyes and tip my head up so that the sunshine kisses my face. I imagine him up there somewhere. I let the music sweep over me. The hairgrip falls to the ground and I don't care. I kick it away.

And then the music stops.

The busker is changing his guitar. I watch

as he starts a new song. Something upbeat. Something I do not recognize. His voice is cracking with the melody. It doesn't suit him. I shift in my seat, feeling uncomfortable again. Stupid even.

My phone buzzes. Frustrated, I dig it out. Open it up. There are two missed calls from Amira and a text. A text from Alfie.

Hey. You OK? Don't rush off like that.
You'll worry me.

I stare at the words, surprised. Seriously? He's that worried? Is he for real? I don't even know how to answer that. I don't think I can right now.

Instead I call Amira back and we talk. I apologize for storming off, blaming stupid hormones and lack of sleep for my crappy mood. Tell her there is nothing to worry about, that I have stopped hurting myself, it was a one-off. And all the time I stare at my fresh cuts.

*

Thread: Grief

I'm starting a new thread on here, because I'm wondering if my cutting is linked to my bad feelings about my granddad's death. We were so close, you know? Like really close. He was so funny and understood me. He made me feel safe. I just can't get how someone can be there one day and not the next.

Anyway. I know that we all have different reasons for why we cut. So maybe this is mine. And I don't know what to do... I can't stop feeling bad about his death. So how do I stop cutting? I hate how it makes me feel afterwards. The guilt and shame is almost as bad as everything else. I feel dirty.

And pls don't tell me to talk to someone. They'll never understand.

In fact, if they knew the truth about Granddad, they would never forgive me.

*

After this post I feel odd, like I'm not sure if I've done the right thing or not. I hit send and then sit for a bit, totally still.

I know one day I will have to face up to all of this. But I'm not really sure I can.

Right now I don't think I'll ever be ready.

Mum was stressed. Christmas always did that to her. I didn't get it. The pub looked excellent – they'd really gone to town with the decorations. And we were shutting for a few hours on Christmas Day so that we could have a proper Christmas dinner. That made a real change.

I was twelve years old and couldn't wait. This would be the best Christmas ever! I'd spent hours looping tinsel over every picture and ornament I could find upstairs. I even twisted a silver vine around the plant. It looked awesome. In the far corner, the tree twinkled. Mum had brought a fancy white one, almost seven feet. She'd spent ages carefully hanging each bauble on the branches, making sure they looked right. I didn't like to help with that bit. I just knew that my clumsy fingers would get it wrong. She'd only end up moving anything I hung up. She thought I didn't notice, but I always did.

Most of the time Mum had been in the kitchen, preparing the dinner. She said she wanted to keep it traditional. This meant a huge turkey was stuffed in the oven and the smell of Brussels sprouts was seeping into the living room. It was a strange, metallic smell that I didn't like much. I kept out of her way. Instead I busied myself with the new phone I'd been given.

My nana, Tessa, arrived first — Dad's mum. She had driven up from Kent with my dad's sister, Yvonne, and her husband, Tony. They came with an armful of gifts and full of chatter. Nana swept me up in one of her big hugs. All I could smell was expensive perfume and big hair. Then she threw herself down on the sofa and demanded a drink. Tony went off with Dad down to the bar and Yvonne chattered with Mum in the kitchen, their soft laughter ringing around the room. I think I was expected to entertain Nana, but I kept my head down, focusing on my present. She always asked the same questions. "What are your grades?" "What are your long-term plans?" and "Why can't you smile more?"

Mum was grumpy and a bit sad. She wanted Gloria there, but had to make do with a phone call instead. "It's not the same," she muttered to Dad, "I need her here."

I willed Granddad to hurry up and come. I

needed him *there*, to liven the place up. It was my idea, him coming. I'd begged Mum to invite him – told him she couldn't *not* include him. When he was in good form, he could light up a room, make us all laugh. Besides, we couldn't have him sitting at home alone. In the end she agreed. "Against my better judgement," she said.

I was so relieved when I heard the side door crash and the sound of his loud voice rattling into the room.

"Ho! Ho! Ho! And a Merry Christmas to you all!" He bounced in, a Santa hat perched lopsidedly on his head, clutching a supermarket carrier bag. He looked red-faced and a bit wobbly. He immediately caught sight of Nana. "Tessa! You're here already and looking as radiant as ever!"

He bent over and swept her up in a hug. She started giggling and mock-protesting. "Oh, you daft bugger! Get off now!"

"Gabi! My best girl. Come here."

I got up, and even though I was pleased he was there, I didn't want to kiss him. I didn't like fuss being made, or any big shows of affection — that wasn't me. But he knew that. Instead I wrapped my arms around his middle. I could smell stale smoke and the malty scent of old beer. He smelt like the pub. I glanced at the bag, expecting him to pull some gifts out, but instead he pulled out a four pack of lager, proudly. Like this was something good.

"Happy Christmas!" he said, and he flopped in a chair. He flipped open a can, making a huge hissing sound and chuckling to himself. There was a pause and then everyone started talking at once, filling the room with a buzz of noise. I moved closer, feeling protective.

Mum walked over to him. "Are you OK, Dad?" she asked him quietly, and her voice sounded odd, wobbly.

"Oh," Granddad laughed. "And you care now?"

"Oh, Dad." Her face crumpled. "Of course I care. I've been trying to call. You can't keep ignoring things."

"I'm ignoring nothing," Granddad muttered, not looking at her.

"And the money?" Her voice dipped lower. "Are you still in trouble? We can't keep bailing you out."

"I don't need your help," he said, taking a longer sip of his drink.

"Dad..."

Granddad just sat further back in his chair. "Happy Christmas, darling daughter! Why don't you stop with the lectures and get on with the dinner?" Then he burped loudly and giggled.

"At least slow down on the drinking..." she whispered, looking furtively at me. "It's Christmas – Gabi's really looking forward—"

"Maybe mind your own bloody business," he said, loudly enough for everyone to hear.

I cringed inside, willing Mum to leave him alone. It was Christmas. I watched her stalk back to the kitchen. Granddad, however, was laughing softly to himself.

Later as we sat down for dinner – the dinner that Mum had spent all day cooking – Granddad refused to move and join us. Instead he kept drinking and singing to himself in that chair. He looked far away and lost. Mum ate in stony silence, her face pinched and tight. We barely spoke. Dad tried to crack jokes and Yvonne and Tony pulled crackers. But Mum and Nana Tessa kept flashing Granddad furious glances.

Later still, Granddad got up suddenly from the chair, took two steps and fell with a crash to the floor, dragging Mum's beautiful white tree down with him. The baubles bounced across the room while Nana Tessa gasped and Dad and Tony tried in vain to pull him up.

Mum just stood there, hands on hips. Then she said, "This is why he doesn't come over for Christmas." She glared at me then – hard cold eyes. Eyes that told me she'd never listen to me again.

CHAPTER
TEN

Today the sunshine has slipped away again. The clouds are hanging low, dark plump pillows in the sky just waiting to burst. The air outside feels thick and oppressive. It desperately needs some rain to lighten it. I wouldn't actually mind if it poured down today. Anything is better than air you can barely breathe in.

I'm sitting on the bench furthest away from the pub, right by the wall. You could never really call this a garden – it's mainly stone and paving slab, but at least where I'm sitting is away from the road and facing the rose bush, which is thick and out of control. I like watching the bees dance in and out, in an almost hesitant way, skipping across the petals and disturbing all the leaves. They never stop though; all the time their wings are moving at speed – life must be a constant blur.

Mum is inside somewhere, keeping herself busy. We are getting quite good at avoiding each other. I honestly feel like she can't look at me at the moment. It's like she's ashamed of me.

"Are you OK?" she'd asked as soon as I'd got up. We both knew what her question meant.

"I'm fine." Which was me telling her that it was over. That there was nothing to worry about.

She just nodded. I understand. It would be so much easier if this was just a phase. Self-harm is not something Mum would want to involve herself in – it's far too messy. It's not something she could ever understand.

My phone is flashing insistently. Online, arrangements are quickly being made. We are due to meet at the park in an hour for a bit and then Freddie wants to talk about the party in detail. I can't believe it's tomorrow; it seems to be on us so soon. Freddie is so excited, his enthusiasm is almost bursting out of my screen.

> This WILL be the best night EVER.
> I WILL be a LEGEND
> You will ALL remember this night FOR
> THE REST OF YOUR LIVES

Everyone is buzzing about it, and even Amira is starting to relax a little. She's starting to think it might – might – be fun. She's got herself a new silky dress that she's bound to look gorgeous in. Part of me wonders whether I should've been braver with my own outfit. I guess I find it easier wearing the same basic clothes. I know they suit me. Why change it?

Separately from the group, I also receive another message from Alfie.

> You OK? Coming later?

As I tap out my reply, I half continue to watch the bees and their frenetic dance. They never seem to tire, they never give up.

And all the time they are buzzing.

I hit the ramp hard with my board. A jolt. I'm nearly knocked backwards, but I hold my arms out. I keep my balance and ascend the other side. I can't fight the grin that's forcing its way out of me. I leap up off the board, punching the air with my fist.

"Yes!"

The perfect air jump. And I did it.

Me!

The guys are cheering and whooping. Freddie is jumping in the air like an absolute loon. "Gabs, that was seriously awesome!"

I turn and grin at them all, adrenaline bursting. My heart is hammering in my chest and my head is giddy with excitement. I'm so pumped I want to do it again and again. I want to freeze that jump and relive it over and over. I grab my board ready to try again, wondering if it could be that perfect – if it's possible to go just that bit slower so I get the chance to really absorb it.

As I move round the ramp, Alfie walks over. His smile is wide and he's shaking his head, like he can't believe what he's just seen. He grabs my arm gently. "Gabs, that was your best ever."

"Thank you."

I feel weirdly shy. He's staring at me all intense; those eyes just seem to lock into mine and make me feel all tingly. I find myself looking at his mouth, at its lovely soft curve. I quickly look away again, not wanting him to see the burning in my cheeks. Not wanting to give away the thoughts I am thinking. The rest of the gang are sitting further off, staring at Freddie's phone; some more party stuff I'm guessing.

"I'm going back up," I say, as casually as I can.

He nods. "OK. I'll watch."

"Seriously? You not coming?"

He shakes his head. "No way, I want to see you do that again."

I move slightly closer to him. The gap between us is suddenly tiny. I can smell him – It's nice, fresh despite the heat. I can see tiny flecks of yellow in those greeny-brown eyes. I can see those eyelashes dead close, so long and ... well, so pretty! My skin prickles. I feel itchy, uncomfortable. I'm not used to this. I'm suddenly aware of myself. Of how tall and awkward I am. How hot and sweaty I feel. Of how messy my hair must look after that jump. And of the marks on my leg.

"Gabs..." His voice is soft. He is leaning in to say something and his eyes are so, so serious. Intense. I want to pull away. I can't stand it. I don't want him saying stuff. Stuff he'll only regret, especially if he knew who I really was. I twist neatly out of his grip.

"What?"

"I just..."

I keep looking at him, studying his face. He's lovely, I realize. There is a part of me, a big part of me, that wants to grab him, pull him into a hug. I bet he feels so nice. I bet kissing him would be so good.

But...

But...

"I really like you, Gabi,"

I like you too. I do.

But...

"Oh, Alfie. That's really sweet ... but..."

I've let the "but" escape. The worst word. I regret it straight away.

I hear his sigh, just a soft breath, but enough. I know he's defeated. "It's OK. I get it."

And I don't know what to do. I don't know how I can be with him – not as I am – but I don't want to mess this up either. I want to get it right.

"Sorry," I say, trying to keep my voice light. "I've just got my mind on this, that's all. But – why don't we talk later? At the party?"

"Yeah, sure." He looks up at me, almost shyly.

"Cool." I smile at him. Show him everything's all right. Because it will be. At the party I will be calmer. I will look good. I will feel better.

"Cool," he says. "Sounds good."

I clatter my board on the top of the ramp and don't look at the guys below me. I don't want to see their faces. Right now, here on the ramp, I feel like I'm entirely on my own, as if no one knows I'm alive. What would that even be like? To no longer exist? To disappear from other people's consciousness? To stop being their problem? I squeeze my eyes shut and for a second I can block out the sounds around me. I concentrate solely on my breathing – in and out, fast and ragged.

It's just me and the board. One jump. I'll be flying again.

I'll be free.

I open my eyes and breathe slowly. I bend, touching the front wheel first – my ritual, my secret agreement between me and the board. *We will get through this.* I let myself go.

I take the jump again, waiting for the clouds to embrace me.

This time I close my eyes.

Thread: Re: Grief

Thanks for the comments, guys. Honestly, I wasn't expecting so many. That makes a lot of sense about counselling. I suppose it's just taking the plunge, isn't it? Telling someone what's going on.

I have a good friend. I could talk to her.

Thing is though – I'm embarrassed. There was someone else we all knew – a girl, sort of on the outside of our gang, and she cut herself. The others used to say really nasty things – you know, calling her attention seeking and stuff. I was just as bad. I thought she was doing it to look cool.

I feel so bad about that now.

And there's this boy. I like him. I think he likes me. But he thought this girl was stupid for what she did. He'd feel the same about me if he knew the truth.

Emski – thanks for commenting. I'm sorry you lost your brother. That must've been awful.

Did you find anything that helped you?

And in answer to your question – yes. I really want to stop.

I need to stop.

Xx

I shut down the site quickly; I never like to be on there too long. I always feel guilty, like I'm admitting to some big, bad thing. I clear my history, like I always do. Then I open Facebook. I bring up Freddie's page. His big, smiley profile picture greets me. Before I can stop myself I click on Freddie's friends. I find her almost immediately, like I knew I would – Freddie befriends everyone.

Fliss.

Her picture is quite an arty one. A black-and-white shot where she is looking down at her hands, she is holding some kind of beaded necklace. I scroll down. More shots.

My stomach lurches. Her arm. Deep cuts – red and deep. Underneath she has typed, "This is what pain feels like." Seventy-eight people have liked the picture. Someone else, a boy called Wez, has called her a freak. Others have told her to get help.

I keep staring at the image. My skin prickles. She has hurt herself badly. In the past I would've laughed at her for posting about it so publicly. But now I just want to sob. To scream. Why are people liking her post? Why is no one helping her?

I push my laptop away and grab my phone. There's a message from Amira waiting for me. It's like we have a psychic force linking us together; we always know when the other is upset. We always have.

I'm so worried about you, hun.
Please let me help you.

I think of her, my best friend. Her kind, gentle way, but underneath it a core of steel. She would understand. She would get what I was going through. All the things we'd been through – she'd be the only one I could really trust.

Maybe I should let her help me.

Maybe it is my turn to lean on her.

Things got worse and worse after that Christmas. They didn't want me seeing him at all. "He's in a bad place, love," Mum would say, her eyes bright but her voice hard. "It won't be good for you to be around him. Believe me, I should know."

"Listen to your mum," Dad would say. "She knows what she's talking about."

I couldn't understand it. This was my granddad. And he wanted to see us. One night he even turned up again at the pub, but Mum turned him away. Told him to go home and sober up. Her coldness was growing; it was like she was turning to ice in front of me.

"But he needs us," I'd say.

"He's never needed anyone," Mum would reply, turning away from me and closing down the conversation immediately.

I hated it. I hated how she was. She was like a stranger now.

The only person I could talk to was Amira.

"How can she do this?" I whispered to her in the safety of my room. "He's her dad."

"Maybe she was embarrassed," Amira suggested. "Maybe she just can't deal with his drinking?"

"I guess," I sighed. "But he's harmless, not evil. Sometimes..." I caught my breath.

Amira stared at me hard, the stare that always got to me, the stare that said I could tell her anything. "Sometimes what?" she said.

"Sometimes I think she ... made him like this. My mum. She doesn't love him. His wife left him. He brought Mum up all on his own and now she won't even speak to him. He ... he must be so lonely. No wonder he drinks sometimes."

"It must have been hard for him," agreed Amira. "Doing it on his own. But maybe he was like this when she was a kid? Maybe he drank too much then?"

"I wouldn't know. She's never talked about her childhood, and when I try she just changes the subject."

"I guess she'll tell you when she's ready."

I shrugged. "But still, she could try harder with him. He's her dad."

"Maybe she wants to," said Amira softly. "But she doesn't know how."

CHAPTER ELEVEN

I can smell singed hair, like burnt butter, in the air. I shift slightly, scared she's going catch my ear, or, worse, the side of my face. God knows why I trusted her in the first place. Anything for a quiet life.

"Keep still! You want this done properly, don't you?"

"I want to keep the skin on my face!" I imagine showing up tonight with red burns down my face. Hardly the look I was going for...

"Ha, bloody ha!"

"Yeah. Well. You might laugh."

The weird thing is, Mum is completely different when she's doing beauty stuff – she goes quiet, just concentrates and gets on with it. I find it a bit unnerving because I'm so used to her talking all the time. Or nagging. Or moaning.

"It's pointless really. You'll never get my hair dead straight. It'll always fight back," I say.

"You just have a little kink in the middle." She nudges the back of my skull with the irons to demonstrate. "Right there. It'll look so glossy and shiny once I've straightened it out." She pauses. "I'd love to have hair like yours. It's so blonde. So long. True Cinderella style."

"It gets in the way. Anyway, what are you on about – you *are* blonde!"

Mum giggles. "Yeah, out of a packet. My hair is normally just mouse. You get this colour from ... well, I'm not sure who..."

"Not Dad!"

We both laugh. Dad is losing his beloved hair – the circle of baldness is becoming clearer by the day. But his hair is very dark, as is most of his family. Granddad had brown, almost sandy-coloured hair. So who did I take after?

"I guess it must be after your nan. My mum," Mum says, softly, pulling on my hair. "I never really knew her of course, but she was blonde. I remember that."

"How old were you when she left?" I ask. I keep my head dipped. I know this is delicate ground. Mum usually changes the subject when it comes to Nan.

"Five. Just five. She just left me with him ... with your granddad. I never heard from her again."

"Do you know why she left?"

The tugging is slightly harder now. Mum sighs. "Who knows? I guess she didn't want to be a wife, a mum? They had their problems... It was a long time ago. I don't like to think about it really."

"But don't you wonder where she is? Where she might be now?"

I look up. Mum is looking straight at me through the mirror. I stare at her huge eyes, heavily lined with black pencil, framed with long lashes. I never really noticed how sad they look – kind of large and lost. She blinks and bites her lip. In

179

the reflection we don't really look like mother and daughter. She's so young, still. I guess we could be sisters, especially now that my hair is as glossy and healthy looking as hers, not hanging round my face. If I wore as much make-up, we'd probably look identical.

"Mum?" I say, trying to wake her up. She looks far away, hair straightener held in mid-air, worried look etched on her face.

"I don't want to talk about this," she says softly. "I don't like to waste my breath on her."

"Mum—"

I long to ask her more. This is her history. Mine too, but already I can see she is shutting down. Her eyes have hardened again.

"Sorry. We need to get you ready. You need to be at Amira's in what? An hour? That's no time at all! You must be so excited. I used to love parties."

She's gabbling again. I watch as she grabs another handful of my hair and draws the irons through.

"Mum? Don't you wonder where she is?"

"No. Why should I? She left us. She left me."

"But she's your mum."

A pause, then the tugging of my hair continues. "And I'm yours. And I'm asking you to stop this now."

"But Granddad must have missed her."

"I guess. He did love her."

"But he never talked about her much either."

"Gabi." Mum touches my head, pulls a lock of hair away from my face. "These are old wounds, long healed up. You're best not picking away at them. We don't want to open this stuff up again."

"I just want to understand."

"There's nothing to understand," she says sadly. "Some things we never will."

I keep looking at my reflection. I guess I look OK. My top is cool. My hair looks longer and under control. My make-up is perfect. I barely recognize myself. I mean, I still look like me, but better. Good, even.

But pouty red lips and heavily kohled eyes don't show the real me. And just because my face looks pretty on the outside, it doesn't mean I'm not ugly.

Only I can really see my true self.

Of course I reach across for my phone. I bring up the camera. Selfie shots in the mirror. I contort my body so that it looks just right. I bend my neck. I need people to see this fresher, newer version of me. They will see it. They will see a girl who's dealing with stuff, coping, getting on. Gabi – strong, confident, a laugh. I keep clicking. So many pictures. When I glance at my screen I have loads to pick from. It takes ages just choose the best two, but I feel a surge of energy. A rush to upload them.

I peer closer at the screen, right into my eyes. I can see some of the pain there, some of the frustration – but only a little. It's hiding inside of me, it bubbles away in my blood – liquid-like, moving through me, filling me up. Suddenly my phone vibrates and buzzes. My virtual world has awoken again and today it's telling me I'm OK. Everyone likes this "me". Everyone.

*

Amira bursts out of her front door and drags me inside. I'm thrown off balance. All the way here I've been wrapped up in my own thoughts. Mainly about Mum, who was nowhere to be found when I left the pub, and her mum, and Granddad. How must she feel now that she's lost both of them? Lonely, probably.

"Gabi, you look amazing! I'm nowhere near ready!" Amira hisses, pulling me through the door, which is weird because she looks ready to me. In fact she looks awesome, in a short red dress and black heels. I find myself yet again wishing I was teeny tiny; next to her, I feel like a gangly freak.

"My face! Look at it!" she shrieks, speeding back upstairs, so I have no chance to even judge. Instead I pop my head round the door of the living room. Amira's mum is curled up on the sofa watching TV.

"Hi!" I wave.

"Gabi! You look gorgeous." Bonita jumps up and walks over to me, gathering me up in a hug. She's tiny just like Amira and very thin. She looks paler today, more tired than usual. I wonder if she's been working longer hours. I always worry that I might snap her in my grip. But her smile is the brightest I've ever seen. "You look like a catwalk model!"

"Don't be daft!" I laugh.

"Seriously. My goodness, you have your mother's beautiful features, plus some. You'll be fighting the boys off."

My thoughts flash to Alfie, which immediately makes my skin prickle. I hate how confused I feel about him. How much I like him, but how I can't let him in. I can't let him know.

There is thundering on the stairs and Amira bursts back in. She looks so wound up. "Mum! I can't get the eyeliner right!" she moans, then she turns to me. "Bloody hell, Gabi – you *do* look amazing. I didn't even notice properly before."

"Mum did my hair, that's all."

"Normally you just look ... well you know, casual." She giggles. "And now I feel even worse because next to you I look like the ugly Smurf."

"Amira! You don't at all!"

I shake my head at her – her make-up is perfect,

as is her hair, and the dress is super cute. Maybe the truth is no one sees themselves like other people do. I take her hand. "Honestly. You look great. Why are you stressing?"

"I dunno. Maybe because it's Freddie's party, I just wanna ... you know, look nice." Amira squeezes my hand back. "Thank you though. Mum, have you got that necklace I can borrow?"

"Oh yes, of course." Bonita smiles at us both and then leaves the room.

"And anyway, what about you?" Amira waggles her eyebrows suggestively. "Playing it cool with Alfie the other day, I hear?"

"What?"

"At the park. According to Freddie he came over to chat to you – to ask you out maybe – and you were really ... well, you brushed him off a bit. He's told Freddie he's not sure whether you're interested or not. I think he's hoping to talk to you tonight."

"I said we could," I say slowly.

"But do you like him?"

"Yes, yes I think so." My tummy flips and twists again. "I was just distracted before, in the park. I was in the middle of a jump. I've got a lot on my mind at the moment. But I do like him."

"Well, maybe you should let him know that."

"What do you mean?"

"I mean he's a nice guy, but he doesn't want to be seen as desperate. If you like him – you better tell him."

"I—"

"Here you go, Amira! Was this the one you wanted?"

Bonita strolls back into the room, holding up a beautiful silver locket, just as I was about to tell Amira that I haven't got a clue what to do.

It was Saturday, late afternoon, and I didn't know what to do.

I had snuck round to see Granddad again. Mum and Dad were clueless about me going. Mum was at the salon again and it was packed in the pub, so Dad was occupied. It had been easy to nip over.

Granddad hadn't been himself for ages, but that day he was worse than usual. He was pacing up and down, muttering to himself, and he kept looking out of the back window in the kitchen. He had to lean over the great pile of washing-up in the sink as he did so. I didn't understand how the pile could have grown so much; there was only one of him after all. I couldn't help but notice the empty beer cans by the bin and a plate of dried-up baked beans left on the table. There was even old dog food ground into the floor. The place was a mess.

"Are you OK?" I asked.

He grunted, pulling back the net curtain, not even looking at me properly. "It's that fella next door – the one with the flash car. He's banging about in the back garden."

I peered over Granddad's shoulder, immediately catching the scent of stale booze and unwashed clothes. Through the murky window, I could see a large man, stuffing things into black bin liners, picking his way carefully across the broken fence between the two gardens.

Suddenly, Granddad brought up his fist and slammed it against the glass, making me jump. "Oi! You! Leave that alone! You're on my property! Get off!"

I had never seen him move so quickly. He sped out of the back door, all the time shouting at his neighbour, who was now looking up, confused. I followed behind, curious and a little scared.

"I never said you could take stuff!" Granddad was shouting, going right up to him and shaking his fist.

The man stepped back a little, shaking his head. "It's a mess out here, mate. My little girl can't play out here like this. You need to fix this fence. It's not safe."

"I told you I'd sort it in my own time," Granddad said. "It's none of your business."

"It's antisocial – all of this," the man flapped his hand at the bags. He looked tired.

"I'll sort it," Granddad muttered, but he didn't sound convincing.

The man poked the grass with the toe of his trainer. "There's glass here. Broken bottles." His eyes caught mine and I saw something glimmer there – sadness? Pity? "You've got kids of your own here too! That's not right. It's a deathtrap! Someone could get hurt!"

I felt a flash of anger. I wasn't a kid! I was twelve!

"You've got no right judging me! Who are you to tell me what to do?" I could hear the slur in Granddad's voice.

"You shouldn't be looking after her! You can barely look after yourself!" the man said, his face all smug and know-it-all. I wanted to slap him; my hands were burning to. "You shouldn't even have that dog. It's barking all night long. You shouldn't have it if you can't look after it!"

"You have no right to say that." I stepped forward, taking Granddad's arm firmly and pulling him towards me. He was surprisingly light and moved easily with me. He didn't resist.

"Are you sure you're OK with him?" The man stepped forward, his face softening a little, but I wasn't interested.

"Keep your fat nose out!" I snapped, and I dragged Granddad away.

I could feel myself shaking, but I kept my head high.

No one put my Granddad down.

No one.

But inside me something new gnawed away – a sense of shame that I couldn't quite ignore.

CHAPTER
TWELVE

We can hear the music as soon as we turn down the street. It already seems to be vibrating through the pavement and bursting out of the walls at the side of the house. Amira has been quiet for most of the way, clutching her coat tightly against her and walking slowly. I can feel how nervous she is.

"Are you OK?" I ask. We are drawing up to the house now. The door stands open, bleeding weak light and noise into the scruffy garden.

"We should've brought something," Amira nudges me. "Shouldn't we?"

A couple of girls barge past me. I vaguely recognize them as friends of Cat. Older and far cooler than us. In their hands they clutch bottles that clink loudly as they walk.

"We'd never have been served," I say.

"You look older, especially tonight."

"No I don't." I shrug. "So what? We turn up empty-handed. It would look worse coming with Coke or lemonade, like it was some kids' party. I don't know what the big deal is – Freddie will have loads inside."

Amira nods, but is still hesitating by the gate, her hand resting on the wall.

"You don't ever drink anyway!" I point out.

"Yeah..."

"Are we going in or what?"

The banging bass seems to be a foreboding. A warning. It's getting louder, I swear. I glance back at Amira and her face looks so pale. Then she nods.

"OK," she says. "Let's go."

The music is so loud in here, like proper hurting my ears loud; I can feel it rumbling through my entire body. I'm in the living room, but it's barely recognizable in semi-darkness, just a mass of moving shapes, dank smells and voices muted by bass. I want to sit down in a corner somewhere. I want to flop. I'm sick of being barged about already. I hardly know anyone here. I lost Freddie and Amira ages ago, and I have no clue where Alfie is.

I feel young and awkward, out of place – clutching a can of warm, flat lager that makes me feel like I've licked out the inside of the pub. All I can smell is the sweet scent of beer.

It reminds me of something else. Or of someone. Someone I'd rather not think about tonight.

The crowd in front of me breaks apart a little. A group of Year Elevens. The girls eye me up. One smiles. It's a smile that does not go past her lips. I know their names, but they are not people who would know me.

"I love your hair," says a girl called Beth. "Do I know you from somewhere?"

"I go to Millbank too. I'm in Year Ten."

"Oh ... yeah. Of course." She smiles again.

Almost a pity smile, like, "Poor you for being so young."

The girl behind her moves forward, shimmering in a short black dress. It's Freya – Alfie's ex-girlfriend. She looks stunning, with bobbed black hair, a heavy fringe and a face that is made-up to cool perfection. I want to hate her, but I kind of love her for looking so good.

"You skate, don't you, with Alfie?" she says. Her voice is raised above the music. "I've heard that you're really good."

"Yeah, I skate," I nod, still feeling awkward. "But I'm not that good, really."

"He talks about you a lot, really rates you. Don't put yourself down."

The other girls have backed off a little now, possibly bored by our conversation. Freya leans in a little. Her voice softens.

"He's a lovely guy, you know? Alfie? I really wished it had worked with us ... but I guess we both don't suit that way. Probably best as mates ... but you two..." Her eyes twinkled.

"What?" I can't help it; I want to hear more about what she thinks of me and Alfie.

"He lights up when he talks about skating and he lights up talking about you. You'd be a fool not to notice."

I clutch my can, not sure what to say. Part of me wants to smile in delight and part of me wants to shake her. To tell her she doesn't know anything. That I'm not the person he thinks I am.

"He's here tonight," she says, smiling. "You should find him. Talk to him."

"I ... I want to. I just..."

Freya gives me a friendly nudge. "Well, why don't you? What have you got to lose?"

I almost snort in her face.

Only someone like her could ask something idiotic like that.

I push my way through hot bodies, longing to find Amira, Cat – anyone who can talk sense for a moment. I head to the kitchen, hearing Mum's voice drifting in my ear: *All the best parties happen there!*" Given the size of Freddie's, I already know that this is unlikely.

One good thing is that it's slightly quieter in here. Dylan and Si are grabbing cans from a box by the door. I thump Dylan's arm, glad to see a familiar face.

"Hey! You seen any of the others?"

He flashes a sly wink at Si, who starts giggling like a loon. I've never told anyone this, but I've always found Si dead annoying.

"Well . . . we saw Freddie and Amira sneaking off upstairs about five minutes ago. So I'm pretty sure what *they're* up to," Dylan says. "I guess we won't see them for a bit..."

"Lucky Freddie!" says Si, giggling again. His beer is dribbling down his chin. Seriously, I don't know why people think he's cool.

I shrug, trying not to look bothered, even though inside I'm surprised. Amira is very private about these things. I know she wouldn't do stuff with Freddie at a party, for everyone to gossip about. At least I'm pretty sure she wouldn't. She was acting weird earlier. Maybe they planned it? Maybe that's why she was so nervous.

"OK, so where's Alfie and Cat? Seen them?"

"Cat's in the garden with a group of girls I've never seen before," Dylan says, looking bored. "And Alfie was here earlier... Not sure where he is now. With Freya? Or maybe looking for you?"

Si starts giggling again. "OK," I say. "Never mind."

My can is empty now, which is weird, because I don't even remember drinking it all. I balance the empty tin on a pile stacked up on the counter and grab another from the box. I don't really want it, but something has to get me through this. I flick open the tab and take a long gulp. It tastes revolting. I know I'm not going to drink much more.

"Nice one!" Si says, raising his can towards mine. We clink our drinks together like the drunks do in my pub and then I move away, back into the hall, trying to ignore that sour taste in my mouth and the empty feeling in my tummy.

I almost walk right into her.

Fliss.

She is standing there, her thin face lit by the light of the downstairs toilet. Her top is sleeveless and you can see the scars on her arms. Her friends cluster around her protectively.

Her eyes catch mine and she smiles. It's almost apologetic. *I'm sorry you had to see this.*

I can't look at her. I can't.

She cuts herself.

Like me.

Just being near her is making me hate her so much. I can't stand this. I can't be here, looking at her. Seeing this. Seeing those scars.

"You stupid bitch," I say.

I was visiting most days after school now. I still liked to check on him, even if it was just for half an hour or so. His house was on the way to the skatepark, and he was one of the few people that would listen when I talked about it. It was nice to tell someone in the family what I was doing. Someone who wouldn't be distracted by another customer, or someone whose eyes wouldn't glaze over the minute I started to speak about skating. At least Granddad attempted to look interested.

"I'm getting really good at ollies now, Granddad!"

"Ollies? What are they again?"

"It's like a jump, with the board. Over something – like steps or grass. It's a pretty basic move but it took me for ever to learn."

"That's great, love, really good. See – you put your mind to it and you can get anything done."

Some days we would sit on the sofa together watching YouTube videos of famous skaters. When they did something amazing I would grab his arm and feel how thin it was. It worried me. But he refused to eat much when I was there. He always insisted he was OK.

"These guys are great!" he would say, pointing at the screen.

"I know. I'd love to be like that. Alfie – he can do tricks like this."

"This Alfie, he sounds good. A bit talented, eh?"

"He's pretty cool."

Granddad smiled. "It's great to be good at something like that. Enjoy it. Embrace it while you can."

I thought of Granddad's car outside, the one he used to spend days doing up. He'd not done anything on it for years. In fact, he rarely moved from the living room. I'd noticed how he was starting to get a weird fat tyre just around his middle. The rest of him was still stick thin. His skin was starting to look shiny and slightly yellow. There was never any fresh food in the house, only tins. And beer. Plenty of beer of course.

"Do you think, maybe, we should start doing that car again? I could always help you," I said.

"Nah... Can't be bothered." He shifted slightly, coughed deep and throaty, and I could hear the mucus moving in his chest. He leant back and lit himself another cigarette. "Maybe next week, eh?"

"Yeah. Maybe next week."

"Put another video on. Let me see what you want to do next."

I uploaded another clip and watched as his expression changed to one of awe and wonder. His lips curled in that soft smile of his and he nodded slightly.

"One day you'll be this good!" he said.

I looked back at the screen, at some guy spinning effortlessly in the air. "Nah, Granddad. I doubt that..."

"Oh yes you will..." He breathed out hard. I could hear the rattle as if some bird was trapped in his lungs. "Gabi. You can do anything."

CHAPTER THIRTEEN

I need a room. A place to escape. I can hear their voices. I can hear Fliss shrieking, "What does she even know about it?" and someone else shouting, "I'll have it out with her, bitch! How could she say that?"

I need space. I need to breathe – to get my thoughts together – and then what? Apologize? Leave?

Something?

I push open a door. A room in darkness.

"Hello?"

No answer.

I slip in.

There is a musty smell in here. A room that's not had its windows opened for a while. I see the bed shape in front of me and I sit on the end. I don't want the lights on. I don't want anyone to see I'm here.

"Gabi?" a voice in the darkness makes me jump. Then I realize it's Freddie.

Immediately I remember that Freddie and Amira came up here before me. I can feel myself glow red. Oh God, what have I disturbed?

"I'm so sorry! I'm going!" I say, moving quickly towards the door.

"It's OK, you don't have to. It's just me."

"Just you?"

"Yeah!" The light suddenly flicks on and when my eyes adjust I see Freddie, standing alone by his window, drinking from his can.

"I thought Amira was up here with you?"

"She was. . ." Freddie sounds far away. He's not looking at me. He's staring out of the window, like he's watching the groups that have formed in the garden. We can hear them shrieking from up here. But somehow I know he can't really see them.

"Freddie, what's wrong?" I say as gently as possibly, walking towards him.

And then, without saying another word, Freddie, tough, cool, joker Freddie, bursts into tears.

We sit on his bed for what feels like ages. Freddie sobbing and sniffing and me just listening and feeling a bit useless, a big long lump sitting awkwardly on the edge of his bed. I've never seen him like this before. I've only ever known Freddie as the cool joker, the laid-back one. The one that makes us all laugh. This is weird and unnerving and I'm not sure how to deal with it. I'm pretty sure he doesn't usually cry like this. Maybe the beer is to blame.

"I want to stop the whole party. Just tell them all to go. How many are my real mates anyway?" he says.

He has a point. I swear I've never seen half the people in the living room before. "Aw, Fred.

You don't mean that. You've been looking forward to this for ages."

"I just wanted something ... you know. Good. Happy. Something to make me feel..."

"What?"

He shrugs, slouching back further on the bed. "I dunno. I'm not sure now."

"What?"

"Things aren't great, you know. Mum and stuff. I've barely seen her. It's just nice having people around me. It makes me forget, I guess." His voice is so sad, so lost.

"I'm sorry," I say.

"It's OK."

"Freddie, where's Amira?" I ask softly.

"She went, about half an hour ago." His voice is sulky now; he won't look at me. "We had a bit of a row..."

"A row?"

My mind is racing now, thinking of Amira. Wondering if she's OK.

"Yeah. It wasn't much. We were talking and

stuff and she just went funny on me. Got all angry. I dunno. . ."

"Why did she get funny? What did you do?"

"Nothing!" he says angrily. "I wouldn't do anything to her. She was in a funny mood."

"She wanted to leave?" I ask.

Freddie sighed. "She barely spoke all night. That's why I brought her up here. I thought we could talk and you know ... I thought maybe I could cheer her up." He buried his head in his hands, till I could only see the thicket of long hair sticking out. "I really like her. I think I might even... I don't want to lose her. I keep screwing everything up."

"I know that feeling. . ." I mutter.

"What?"

"Never mind. Listen – she does get stressed out, Fred. And parties aren't her thing. I think she keeps a lot from you."

"She shouldn't. I love her as she is. She means the world to me. I just keeping getting it wrong, thinking I can joke my way out of stuff!"

We sit for a bit, not talking. I don't think either of us wants to move. I listen to the sounds of laughter downstairs, occasional shrieks.

"I'll text her," I say eventually, getting out my phone. "Make sure she's OK."

Freddie says nothing

I groan as I type. "I think I've upset someone too, Fred."

"Yeah? Who?" He lifts his head, his face is blotchy. His hair all over the place.

"Fliss. I called her a stupid bitch."

Freddie looks stunned. "Er. Why?"

"Because ... because she was flashing her arm around. Her scars. You know, making a big deal out of the fact she cuts."

Freddie rubs his face, pushes back a load of hair that has fallen forward. He looks like he's just climbed out of a hedge. Or a bin. "You shouldn't get on her case, Gabs. She's been through a lot."

"She seems to like the attention."

"Yeah, well maybe she does. Maybe she needs it." Freddie sighs. "Things are pretty messed up for

207

her. She needs help, not girls like you judging her."

"I'm not judging her."

"Really? Seems like it from here."

"I'm not! How can *I*...." The words leave my lips. I flinch, turn away.

"Exactly. How can *you*?"

He can't know. Unless... But she wouldn't. Would she?

"Did Amira tell you?" I ask softly.

"Tell me what?"

"Freddie, stop messing with me. You know what I'm saying."

He snorts. "If you mean your arm, no, she didn't tell me. I saw it. Your sleeves ride up when you skate sometimes. Alfie saw it too. We also see you flinch when you jump. We're not dumb, Gabs."

I say nothing. I feel heavy, like I'm sinking in the bed.

"I'm not judging," he says. "We all have our stuff to deal with."

"Alfie knows?" I say flatly. A rain of ice floods my stomach.

"I think so."

So that's it then. He'll know what a mess I am. Lovely Alfie. My chance. Gone.

"It doesn't matter, Gabi. We're your mates. None of this matters. We just want to help you."

I don't want to cry, I really don't, but my head is ready to explode. I sniff and make a sound like a gasp. The tears that follow seem to come from nowhere. I am shaking, gasping – drowning in my own body. Freddie pulls me towards him. Holds me tight. Rocks me slightly. I can smell that beer. So familiar, deep and yeasty.

Granddad – all I want.

I'm so sorry.

I just wanted to tell you...

I bury my head in his body, try to stop the sobbing – but it's hard, too hard. But in the end there is nothing left and he is just holding me really tight. The two of us. "Thank you," I say, looking up at his sweet, stupid face.

He pushes my hair away from my wet cheeks. "You have snot coming out of your nose," he says, frowning. "It's disgusting."

And it's at that moment, just as Freddie's hand is against my face, and I'm looking up at him, curled in his other arm, trying to decide whether to laugh or punch him – it's at that moment that Alfie walks into the room.

He was asleep when I walked in, TV blaring. I didn't even attempt to wake him. He looked kind of peaceful, spread out on the sofa – the TV remote balanced delicately on his tummy.

It was weird though. Even with the noise of the TV it was too quiet. And then I realized what it was. Weller hadn't even bothered to bark, he was curled up on his bed, by the door. He raised his head and peered at me with sad, dark eyes. Then he buried his muzzle again under a paw.

I walked over to give him a fuss. He seemed smaller somehow and his coat left a greasy film on my hand.

"You OK, boy?" I said.

He blinked and sighed, and buried his head deeper into his body. Normally he liked a fuss, but I got the feeling that today he wanted to be left well alone. Instead I made sure his water bowl was clean and put out some food for him. All the time, Granddad continued to sleep.

"Weller doesn't look well, Granddad," I said, loudly.

"He's fine..." he muttered, not opening his eyes. Sleeping on.

There was still washing in the sink. Plates and cups. He couldn't have much clean stuff to use. I sighed, thinking about his ragged, catchy breath and hacking cough. I had time before I met the others, so I quickly started to wash-up, trying not to gag as I scraped old congealed food into the bin, or watch as small flecks of old food dribbled down the plughole.

I didn't want to do it, but I had to. That pile would keep growing otherwise. Behind me the letterbox rattled. Someone was at the door. Weller groaned in his bed – like he was complaining, "Please, go away. Leave us."

I wiped my hands on the only thing available. It wasn't much of a tea towel and it had a suspicious-looking burn in the middle, but it had to do. I peered through into the living room; Granddad still lay asleep. Weller looked worried, like he was begging me to sort it all out.

I walked over to the front door and looked through

the criss-crossed glass, where I could see the shadow of the caller standing behind. They rattled the letterbox again. Louder this time. It made me cross.

I pulled open the door, peered round.

A man stood there. Not that old. Short, scraggy brown hair and piggy eyes. He was wearing a brown leather coat that was far too big for him.

"Can I help you?" he asked.

"Is Mr Reynolds there?"

I hesitated. I didn't want to wake Granddad up again; he'd be in a right mood. Besides, this man looked annoying. He was bound to be calling about something pointless.

"He's not well. I'm his granddaughter. Can I help?"

"You can give him this," the man said, shoving a fat brown envelope in my hand.

As soon as he did I felt a spark, like a burst of pain. This was not good.

"What is it?"

"I'm from the housing department. Your grandfather hasn't being paying the rent and he's months in arrears. Tell him to read this and get in contact. It's really important he calls the council to discuss this, otherwise—"

His voice hung in the air between us. He blinked and went to move away.

"Otherwise what?"

"Just makes sure he gets the letter. It's important."

He smiled at me. His teeth were short and stumpy and looked odd in his large mouth. I watched as walked away, twisting himself past Granddad's old car and bashed-up paving slabs.

"Thanks," I said.

He didn't turn around. He pushed hard on the gate and made it shake in the post. Behind me Weller and Granddad slept on.

CHAPTER FOURTEEN

"Oh, I'm sorry. I didn't realize I was disturbing you," Alfie says. His voice is cold. Too cold. He walks straight out again, letting the door slam behind him.

For a moment I want to laugh, a totally nervous reaction. This is crazy, like a film or a naff soap opera. How is this happening to me?

Freddie jumps up, muttering under his breath. His hair and his face look even crazier than normal. Jesus, he looks guilty. I go to grab him, to tell him to calm down, but he shakes me off.

This is insane.

"Hey, mate! Wait up!" he shouts and goes after Alfie.

I wipe my snotty, tear-streaked face against the sleeve of my top. Disgusting, but I'm beyond caring. I feel odd, a mixture of numbness and guilt. But we did nothing wrong. We were just talking.

Outside the room I hear shouting. I walk across and peer through the door. Alfie is on the stairs. I don't recognize him like this – his face is white, all clenched up and ugly. He looks like he wants to punch someone.

". . . yeah, Amira would love to hear that, Fred!" he's saying. "I'm sure she'd really understand that."

"Don't be daft. Gabi was upset. We were just—"

"Yeah, yeah. Don't talk crap, mate. I've had it with you. And her!" Alfie suddenly turns, sees me looking through the door. "What is it with you anyway, Gabi? I'm obviously not good enough, so you hit on my mate instead. Nice move. Classy."

"I didn't. . ." I say, my words sounding weak and flat. I step forward but I'm wobbling. I feel like the entire party has quietened, everyone is listening. Even worse, I've spied Fliss staring up at us from the bottom of the steps, all wide eyed and shocked.

"Alfie. Man. Just listen. Let's go back in my room and talk about this," Freddie says.

"We were just talking!" I say, louder now. "Freddie was upset."

Freddie flashes me a look, a kind of "shut up" frown, so I quickly back down. I'm guessing he doesn't want the party to know that he's the sobbing type.

"That was good of you," Alfie says. His words are so cool. I feel like each one is striking me. "I could see how close you both were."

"It's not like that..." I sound like I'm whining now.

"Nah, I'm done," Alfie says. He looks at me with disgust, and my whole body feels like it's been set alight right in front of him. I'm burning here. I'm burning up right in front of him.

"You know, Gabi, I really liked you. I thought you were ... just the coolest girl. Interesting. Talented. Awesome at skating. A good laugh. And I felt sorry for you, losing your granddad and everything. I thought I could help you." He shrugged. "Do you know what? This is probably for the best. I don't need someone as messed up as you. You and Freddie suit each other."

His words fly and hit again. Harder now. I can't reply. I just stand there, taking it. He shakes his head and goes back down the stairs. Freddie follows, shouting protests, but I'm not listening any more.

I felt sorry for you. . .

That's it, isn't it? He pitied me. Poor messed-up Gabi. Lost her granddad and couldn't cope. Started cutting herself.

Well, maybe he's not the nice guy I thought he was.

Maybe I am better off without a jerk like that anyway.

I take a long shaky breath and then move down back towards the stairs. I'm glad it's dark in here. I'm glad no one can really see me. I must look awful.

Fliss is still at the bottom. Her eyes glint at me as I pass.

"Going already?" she says coolly.

I don't reply.

"You were bang out of line earlier," she says. "You know nothing about me."

"I'm sorry," I mutter, pressing past her. "I was angry. I shouldn't have said that."

"You don't understand."

"But I do," I say, walking away towards the front door, and not daring to look back.

Dad would go mental if he knew I am walking back late by myself, but I can't face calling him. Instead I try and call Amira but her phone is turned off.

We need to talk.

I message her, praying she doesn't hear the gossip before we can actually speak.

The evening is still warm and it's not so dark, even though it must be after eleven. I like the streets at this time. I like walking past houses all locked away at night. I imagine the people inside. Some still watching TV, dazed by the bright glowing lights. Others settled in bed. I guess it's strange that I hate night at home, in my own room – trapped with my stupid thoughts – but out here, it's fine. I feel calmer. Everything is quieter and muted.

I just wish I didn't feel so sad.

I turn down my street. Past the shops, all closed now of course. The metal security screens are pulled down and the lights are off. There is no one here. I pause for a second outside Del's, looking at the sign where I jumped up in front of Amira. I remember her shocked face when she saw my arm.

I wish she was here with me now. What would we be doing? Moaning about the party. About how out of place we felt. Amira would be casual about it all. She'd shrug, say, "Never mind – at least we tried." At least we attempted to be like everyone else. Because we were good at that. We were good at fitting in. Being like everyone else. Only I knew how much Amira struggled with her anxiety, with her shyness. And only Amira knew...

Oh God, I want her now.

If we'd stuck together at the party I'd never have ended up in Freddie's room, listening to his drunken sobs, and I wouldn't have shouted at Fliss. Everything would've been fine. I would've left with my best friend at the end of the night. But now everybody hates me.

Oh God. I suck in a breath. A flashback – the thought of Alfie's angry face. He got it all wrong. All of it. And if Amira believes it – believes him instead of me – it will be awful. Just awful.

I feel rooted here. Staring at the shop front. Remembering all the times as a kid, how I'd come here to buy sweets. How I'd come with Granddad and wait outside while he bought his cans.

And now he's gone. And he'll never be back. And I'll never, ever have the chance to tell him the things I need to.

I'll never have the chance to make things right.

I slump against the railings. I'm finding it so hard to move. I'm not sure I want to go home, but I know I have to.

I kick against the railings. Hard. They rattle and shake.

"It didn't have to be like this," I shout.

I kick again. "You didn't have to do this to me!"

I smash my fist down on the hard metal; the impact jars. Fresh pain. Fresh feelings. Burning. Rawness. A new feeling – rage. It's coming from the pit of my stomach. I can still feel the waves of pain, but there's fire there now, roaring inside me, igniting every bit of me. I lift my hand. I can barely see in the dim light, but I can feel wetness. I flex and there is the bite of pain.

What is happening to me?

I creep through the back door, my entrance disguised by the noise of the pub. Saturday night is as busy as always, so they'll be distracted. They won't expect me home for ages; I was meant to be coming back with Amira and her mum. It was all planned. They have no reason to worry about me.

I pause on the stairs, listening to the familiar noises. The music. The clink of glasses. The voices.

And I remember that as a kid I loved that – the sound of the pub's collective voice, its highs and lows, the way you could just about pick out a single word or two. It was almost melodic and so familiar, knowing the exact same people were standing behind those doors, drinking, laughing, sharing stories. Vocal warmth coming through the walls.

Dad once told me you could never be alone in a pub.

Dad always gets stuff wrong.

I creep upstairs and slip into our flat. My hand is throbbing badly now. I turn on the light and force myself to inspect the damage. The knuckles glare red at me, swollen and shiny. A cut runs between them. More blood. More pain. It burns sharply.

I flex my fingers again and cry out in pain – no, this is bad. It really, really hurts.

Tears in my eyes, I walk to the kitchen sink. I run the tap cold and force my fist under the stream of ice. I gasp, biting my lip.

"Oh God..." I mutter, biting harder and tasting blood. "Oh God. Oh..."

The water bounces off the red skin. My skin, bruised and battered, damaged again, like everything I have. All damaged. All ruined.

I'm forcing back the tears, but it's so hard. I just want to sob. I want to sob and never stop. And meanwhile the pain doesn't stop. What good does any of this do?

She comes out from the shadows. Where has she been? Has she been sitting in the darkness, watching me?

"What have you done this time?" she says. Her voice calm, but so quiet I can hardly hear her.

I haven't got the energy for defensive attacks or sharp remarks. I'm too tired. And too sore.

"It hurts, Mum. It hurts so bad."

I show her my hand. And then I cry.

The phone rang.

Hardly anyone calls the phone in our flat. Family and friends use our mobiles, and Dad's business contacts ring the pub. The only people that use the main phone are sales people – and Granddad. So when it rang I saw Mum's eyes jump straight to it

"Answer it, then!" Dad was doing paperwork at the table, which always stresses him out.

Mum sighed and lifted the handset. Then she sighed again. "Dad? OK ... OK. Calm down."

I watched her. She doesn't tend to change her expressions much – she keeps everything locked inside – so her face was calm. But she was twisting the lead of the phone between her fingers.

"OK ... so exactly how is that Gabi's fault?"

I took a step forward. Mum's eyes caught mine.

"Oh, but that's crazy. And not her fault." Mum turned her back away from me. "Will you stop shouting at me?"

I was frozen to the spot. Why was he cross with me? What had I done?

"Dad ... she's done nothing wrong. Now, if you

want to talk then why don't you call back when you're . . . when you're sober!" Mum hissed the words, slammed down the receiver, and then remained with her back to me. Her head was dipped and her hands were hanging loosely to the sides. I could see one hand was curled slightly in a grip.

"He's getting worse. . ." she whispered.

"Is he OK?" I asked.

Mum turned. Her face was deathly white and her eyes were blazing. "Gabi, were you at Granddad's this week?"

"Yes." I hang my head – I know she doesn't want me there. "I went the other day. He . . . he was asleep."

"Asleep? Unconscious more like," she muttered. "Did someone come by with a letter?"

"Yes! I left it out for him. Was that . . . was that wrong?"

She shakes her head wearily. "That letter was an eviction notice."

Dad pushes back his chair and comes towards her. "Oh, love. Come here."

"A what?"

"A letter telling him that if he doesn't get his act together he's going to lose the house." Mum let out a strange noise from her throat. "Oh God, then what? Jack! He couldn't live here. In a pub!" She let out a sudden laugh.

"Why not?" I said.

"Gabi! It's a pub. Think about it. Grow up. You're fifteen now!"

Dad wrapped Mum in his arms. "I'll sort it out. I'll contact the council, explain the situation. How much does he owe this time?"

"We can't keep bailing him out," Mum sobbed. "We'll have nothing left at this rate. We're already—"

"He's your dad. We'll do what we have to do!"

"I'm sorry," I said. "Is he angry with me? Shouldn't I have taken the letter?"

"He's angry at himself," Mum muttered. "He can just never bloody see it."

CHAPTER FIFTEEN

I wake up late. I know it's late because the sun is streaming through the window and it's noisy downstairs. The Sunday trade. I can smell roast dinners being prepared in the main kitchen. Usually this makes me hungry, but today I just feel sick. The thought of eating anything makes my empty stomach churn.

I roll on my side. My hand is neatly bandaged. I stare at it, remembering Mum's careful work, her soft touches and murmured reassurances.

"OK. You can bend it? That's good. I'll clean it and strap it for now... See how it is in the morning. Then we'll talk."

"... *don't say anything. Not now. Not right now.*"

"*Don't get upset. We'll talk again in the morning.*"

I sigh, the heaviness falling deep inside me, a bottomless pit. I picture all the unwanted stuff, all the negative thoughts swimming around inside me, making me constantly uneasy. I don't want to talk. Not now. Not ever. I have nothing to say. Nothing that anyone would want to hear anyway...

Beside me my phone blinks. Messages. I reach for it, stomach twisting, sour taste on my tongue. I remember how I left the party. I'm scared of what I'll find.

The first message is from Freddie.

> Are you OK? Don't worry, I'll sort all of this.

Another from Freddie.

> Are you home? I'm worried. Alf is mad. I will work on him. Can't get hold of Ami. So much for party of the year...

Another from message from Cat, sent later last night.

> Hey hun. Didn't see you go? Loads being said about last night? What happened? Ring me? xx

There were no messages from Amira. I stare at the screen like I'm willing this to be different, then I send her another text, begging her to reply. If she doesn't, I will have to go and see her.

Oh God... I sink back on the bed, phone still clasped in my hand. I don't want to do it, but I do anyway: my finger is already searching for posts, updates, messages. Thankfully there isn't much. A few people have posted on Freddie's wall thanking him for a great (?) night. A few more have posted on Fliss's asking if she's OK, one girl telling her not to take any notice of that "mad cow, Gabi".

Nice.

Alfie's wall is blank; he hasn't posted since the

party. Neither has Amira. In the cyber world they are absent, unobtainable. Lost.

I close my eyes, clench my fists and immediately recoil as the pain from last night's injury floods through me again.

I let the phone fall to the floor. I don't want to see it again.

Mum walks in as I'm getting dressed. I think she probably knocked, but I'm so lost in thoughts I didn't notice. She has tea in her hand and a worried smile on her face. I note the lack of make-up and her scraped-back hair. She's obviously not working behind the bar today.

"I'm glad you're up," she says, placing the cup down and then sitting on my chair, right beside me. "We need to talk."

"Do we?"

"Yes. You know we do."

"What about?"

She gives me a long look. "How's your hand?"

I glance down, trying to ignore the throb. I

feel like it's three times the size. "It's fine," I lie, flexing it to show her that everything is normal. I'm not used to having her in my room. Usually she's in her space and I'm in mine. That's how we deal with stuff. That's how it's always been.

"I'm making you a doctor's appointment," she says. Her voice is calm and even, her eyes carefully examining me, waiting for a reaction. "On Monday. I'm calling them. We need to talk to someone about this, about all of this."

"About what?" I keep my voice cold. "You're mad. There's nothing wrong. I don't want to talk to some doctor."

"Nothing wrong..." she laughs, hollow and short. I see her hands are fiddling with the fringe of her top and I remember them twisting the phone cord that night Granddad rang. "Nothing wrong, Gabi? Can't you see that *everything* is wrong?"

Everything? I shake my head numbly. I don't know what she means.

"You're not right at the moment. Moody, angry... I don't know. And the injuries. You keep..."

"Keep what?"

"You keep hurting yourself. What is it for? Attention? Do we not give you enough, is that it?"

"You're crazy!" I say again. "It was just once or twice. You're wrong."

"Am I?"

She jumps up, pulling up my sleeve before I can stop her and examining the scars – old marks, still red, still reminders. "You think I don't see!" she hisses, her face so close to mine I can see the fine lines around her eyes. "First your arms, then your legs and now your hand. It's not . . . well, it's not normal, Gabi!"

Normal. The word floats there. I want to laugh – I want to shake her off me and say, "Why, thanks for telling me something I don't know, Mum," but somehow – for some reason – the words aren't there. Instead I turn away from her.

Silence. Steady beats. I can hear the clock ticking. The bar sounds downstairs. Mum's ragged breath.

"I'm sorry. I didn't mean that," she says.

I stare at the window, at the bright blue sky, clouds like tiny white whispers drifting across the top. A perfect day to skate, to be at the park away from this. Except now – with everything that's happened at the party – I don't know if I'll ever go back there. "This has been since he died, hasn't it?" she says, quieter now. "You're not coping. You're not dealing with it properly."

"You know nothing," I snap.

"He was my *dad*."

"You keep saying that."

"So, try and understand. It's hard for me too."

I suck in air, that bitter taste again. My throat twists and tightens. I spin around fast. "Hard for you?" I spit, shocking myself at the coldness in my tone. "Hard for you? You HATED him. You did everything you could to make his life a BLOODY MISERY!"

Mum doesn't move. She doesn't scream back; she barely reacts. Then, ever so slowly, her head drops. Her entire body seems to slump in front of me. "You don't understand. You could never understand."

"You never cared. Even now, it's like he never existed."

"Of course he existed," Mum says, her voice soft.

"I know he wasn't perfect, but who is? Who, Mum?" I say, the rage building, sweeping through me. "I didn't care that he drank sometimes. All I know is that he had time for me. He listened. He loved me—"

My voice breaks, words catching, tumbling in my throat. The force of tears sweeps through me. I'm gasping, choking. Mum reaches for me but I push her away. I stagger instead to the window, gripping the sill, feeling myself tipping and sinking.

"Gabi—"

"Please. Go."

"Gabi." Her voice is louder now. Firmer. "Gabi, listen to me."

I squeeze my eyes shut, salt settling on my lips and lingering on my tongue. I am still shuddering, trying to stop the awful sounds, the brutal sobs from escaping my body. I don't like this – all my sadness all on show, all outside of me. It is ugly, undignified, cruel.

"Gabi!"

"What?" I gasp.

"I hate having to think about my life, before...
It's hard for me. I've shut a lot of it away."

"What was hard, Mum? What?"

"Everything. I didn't have a mum. She walked
out on both of us, you know. And me and your
granddad, we didn't get on – so I had to move out.
It's just how it was. We couldn't make it work. I
wanted it to. I loved him so much. But he couldn't
be the dad I needed. Not once she'd left."

I look at her, her drawn face. She looks smaller
somehow.

"Why did your mum leave? What happened?"

"I don't really know." Mum's voice is so soft, I
can barely hear her. "I was told that she couldn't
cope after I was born, that she changed a lot. I
think Dad thought she'd be OK in the end – that
she'd get better – but I guess things got worse."

I stare at her, waiting for her to continue. She
is picking at her nails, looking beyond me at a spot
on the wall. "She never got better, not really. Dad
was working away then. He had some job selling
motors up north, so he was never there. Anyway,

one day she just walked out of the house, leaving me alone. I was three. . ."

"She left you? On your own?"

Mum is very still; her voice is weirdly matter of fact. "I was OK. Well obviously I was – I'm here now, aren't I? The neighbours heard me crying. Social services were called. Anyway, they tried to find her, but no one ever heard from her again. I have no idea where she went, but she obviously wanted nothing more to do with me. With either of us."

"Mum—"

Her eyes suddenly flash back to life and she shudders. I see her whole body stiffen. "Enough of this now. I told you, Gabi. I'm not going through this again. It's history. It's over. I've said enough."

"But . . . but what about Granddad?"

I'm expecting coldness, but not the sudden howl that erupts from her. I almost stumble backwards.

"But *Granddad*? But Granddad *what*? *What about me*?"

Then she flies from the room, slamming my door behind her.

Maybe Mum had been right; maybe I should have left him alone. It was getting harder. I had to force myself through the gate, make myself push open the door. Each time I came my stomach would sink a little, never quite sure what I'd find.

And it was pretty clear that things weren't OK. They were very far from OK.

He stood, swaying slightly in the archway of the door to the kitchen, a can clasped so tightly in his hand I thought he might squash it. A sign of strength, I guess. But in many ways he looked like a fragile butterfly caught in a trap, with his thin lurching body, reedy arms and legs that seemed unable to support him.

"He's dead," he muttered. His words were flat and stretched out. His free hand grabbed the door frame; if he hadn't I think he would have fallen right in front of me. "He's dead now. My little Weller. He's left me. Another one gone."

"Oh no. Granddad, I'm sorry."

I looked at his face, at his unshaven cheeks, at once hollow and swollen, at his yellowing eyes.

Greasy hair stuck flat to his scalp. He looked so frail.

My eyes drifted to Weller's empty bed and a strangled sob caught in my throat. That lovely dog. I would miss him so much. Tears prickled.

"He was old. Too old." Granddad swaggered towards the sink. I saw another four pack there, waiting for him. I also saw the uneaten cereal, growing crusty in the bowl, and a pint of milk slowly warming by the window. He popped the ring pull on the can.

"Do you think you should—"

He laughed, and then coughed, dry and raspy. His body shook with the force of it. He reached forward and leant against the sink, his shoulders bent over. I could see the stains on his jumper, the jumper I knew he had been wearing the last time I was there. "You sound just like her. Like your bloody mother."

"I just think," I took a breath and stepped forward. "I just think … maybe… Granddad, this place is a state. You're not looking after yourself – or anyone else. I told you Weller looked poorly and you ignored me."

"Oh, so you know it all now!" His voice sounded

like it always did, as though his tongue wasn't moving as it should, but the tone was different that day – icy, cold, nasty. The words stung me.

"I just think—"

"What?" He was facing me now. "What do you 'just think'? Hmmm? What is your 'smarty pants' opinion?" He threw up his arm. "Coming over here. Getting under my feet. Do you think I need that? Eh? Do you think I need you here all the time? Snooping around? You nearly got me bloody evicted!"

"That's not fair." I tried to keep my voice calm but I could hear the wobble.

"What is fair? Nothing ever is." He took a loud swallow of drink and then moved towards me. "Everyone I love goes in the end." He smiled, but it wasn't a nice smile. "And you! Little Gabriella. You! I really thought you might be different – that you wouldn't – what's the word now..."

"Granddad, please sit down." He was staggering and beer was going everywhere.

"Judge! I didn't want to be judged. Especially not by you!"

"I don't judge you, Granddad."

"But of course you do, sweetheart. Do you think I'm stupid? Do you think I don't have eyes?" He gestured towards his face, more beer spilling. "And that's why you come here all the time. You come to spy on me, for that mother of yours. You report back. You tell her how bad I am! Because of you, I doubt your precious mother will take me in, will she? I'll be homeless on top of everything else."

"I don't spy on you! Granddad – I love being with you. I love being here."

"Really?" He was sneering now. "You really love spending your time with an old drunk?"

"I love being with you." I tried to keep my voice steady.

"Yeah ... Yeah..." He was pacing again, not listening. Beer glistened on his lips.

"I just worry. I worry that you drink too much. You don't need to. You don't. We care about you—"

He slammed the can down hard on the side and roared with laughter.

"Really?" he said. "That's a funny one."

"We just worry about you," I said softly, feeling lame and clumsy and stupid all at once.

"You all want to change me, that's what. You can't bear to be related to a drunk. An embarrassment." He swayed on the spot, wiping his mouth. "You're just like her. You're just like your mum."

It's like he struck me. He might as well have done.

"Granddad—"

"Just go," he said coldly. "Crawl back to your smug little family. I don't want you here any more. I'm better off alone than with someone who's ashamed of me."

"You can't think that," I said, shock and hurt pulsing through me with every heartbeat. "How can you say these things?"

"Just go, little girl! Run back to Mummy," he said. "I've had enough of you now."

So I did.

CHAPTER SIXTEEN

When she opens the door I want to cry. I want to fall in her arms and howl like a baby. But I don't quite dare. I don't know how she feels about me this morning. So I just stand there awkwardly.

She looks different today; her hair is pinned away from her face, making her look more exposed and vulnerable somehow. She's dressed casually in a tracksuit, which isn't like her. If I didn't know her better, I'd think she was ill.

"Please can we talk?" I ask.

Thank God, she agrees. A nod, that's all. She leaves me for a second to tell her mum and then comes back out, pulling the door shut gently behind her.

We walk slowly down her street. It's odd, the silence – I'm not used to it. I have so much to say but I don't know where to begin – my tongue feels lodged in my mouth.

"I'm sorry I left," she says finally. "Are you mad at me? I shouldn't have walked out like that."

"Left?" I turn to her, confused for a second. "What – the party? Why did you? I was worried."

Amira sighed. "You know what I'm like. I get so nervous at big parties – all day I'd been stressing about it. And then when I got there Freddie was being a complete idiot, trying to get me to drink – nagging me and stuff..." she paused. "I was quiet, he could see that. We went upstairs and I wanted to talk properly, but all he wanted to do was kiss and talk about crap. I wasn't in the mood, so we rowed."

"He seemed upset after. I think... I think he regretted not listening." I hesitate, desperate to tell her everything, but also afraid.

We turn down the path into the side street.

Opposite us there is a large stretch of grass surrounded by trees. As kids we used to play here, making camps and hunting for treasure. It used to seem magical then, but now I can see it for what it is – rotting wood and sprawling bushes. There is a low crumbling wall at the far end. Amira sits down and I join her. She folds her arms against herself, and turns a little so she's facing me. I see she's chewing her lip. That thing she always does when she's nervous, or thinking stuff through.

"I dunno. I was in a foul mood anyway after Dad had wound me up earlier and I just wanted to talk to Freddie. But he was just not listening. I don't think he would do that normally, but he was drunk, Gabs, and acting dumb. I was angry. I had to get out of there. He was doing my head in."

"Why didn't you find me? You could've talked to me. Or I'd have come home with you, you know that."

"I couldn't see you, so I went outside to call you and some idiot got in my way and barged me by the door. I tripped and smashed my phone on the path. He just laughed in my face!"

"Oh, Amira!" Relief floods through me. Her phone was broken! That was why she hadn't replied to me. I wondered if she knows about anything else that happened that night? I have to tell her.

"You know how much that phone cost my mum. I was even more stressed then and upset – so I just went. I'm sorry. I just didn't want to go back inside. I wanted to be home anyway. I didn't want Freddie finding me, and me saying something I'd regret. I just wanted to cool down. And I figured Freddie would've told you that we rowed and you'd work it out. I'm sorry I left you there."

"It's OK."

"No, it's not. I shouldn't have gone in the first place. I knew I wouldn't enjoy it. I was already in such a mood. Dad had made my mum cry before you got there, shouting down the phone at her about maintenance again, so I was stressing about that. I wanted to explain to Freddie and he was completely not listening." Amira sighs. "You get it, you're one of the few people that do. I feel like I have to put on an act for him. A different face.

Make out I'm someone I'm not. I just wanted to him to understand that I find stuff like parties hard. That when my mind's occupied with other stuff and it can be a bit ... well, overwhelming."

"He would understand, too," I say. "If you gave him the chance."

"He does," Amira says, smiling a little. "I spoke to him about an hour ago. I've never known him come round so early – that's why I look so rough!" She laughs. "Anyway, we talked it through and he does get it. He feels awful; he never meant to upset me. I think he regrets the party too, now. He thought it would make him Mr Popular, but instead it's wrecked his house! Someone even spilt beer over their new TV. His mum is going to totally freak."

"Poor Freddie."

"I know. He is lovely really. A bit daft sometimes, but lovely," she says, blushing slightly.

"That's good to hear." I pull her into a hug. "I'm so pleased for you."

"And he told me about Alfie," she says gently. I pull away slightly to look at her face, but she's still smiling. "You don't need to worry, Gabs. I trust you. I know you'd never do anything with Freddie – besides, he's totally not your type! Alfie should know that too. He's being such an idiot."

Relief washes over me. I don't have to confess anything; she already knows and she doesn't blame me. "I just wish he'd listened to us," I say. "I would never do that to you. Freddie was upset about you leaving, that's all. And we were talking about ... other stuff."

"About you hurting yourself?" she says softly.

I take a deep breath. "Yes. It turns out they all knew all along."

She pulls me tight into a hug again. I can smell her clean clothes, her herbal shampoo – the lovely sweet smell of her. I love her so much. She is one of the best things in my life.

"We worry about you, Gabs. You've not been the same since your granddad died. I really think you need to talk to someone. Someone who can help you with your feelings. Don't you think it would help you?"

She means go for counselling – like the people in the chatroom were talking about. Like Mum wants me to.

"Maybe. I don't know."

We sit silently for a bit. I kick my legs against the wall, picking at a loose thread on my top. Amira is very still.

"I just don't understand – *why* do you do it? How does it help?" she asks finally.

"It just does." I stare at my hands, trying to put it into words. "For that split second it's like a release. It's like all the pressure inside me goes away. I can't explain it very well – but somehow it helps, temporarily, like a distraction." I swallow. "And then after – I feel just as bad again."

"But you can't go on like this."

"I know. My mum wants me to go to the doctor. She wants me to stop."

"Will you?"

I stab my foot into the grass and watch as a crescent of mud forms against my shoe. "I don't know," I say eventually. That's the most honest answer I can give. I don't want to lie to her now. Not any more. "Mum told me some stuff last night," I continue. "I'm still getting my head round it. It sounds like she had a pretty hard childhood. Her mum left when she was a baby, practically. And now she's shut away in her room not talking to me."

"That sounds awful. Your poor mum. Do you think she'll talk later?"

"I doubt it. I think she hates me for bringing it all up."

"Of course she doesn't hate you, Gabs. It must just be hard for her."

"I guess. But she's still so angry with Granddad and I don't get that. I know he drank a bit – well, a lot towards the end – but he was still a human being. He was good to me, you know? He was like—"

"A dad?" Amira says softly.

I think of my own dad and want to sob with frustration. "Granddad always had time for me. We had a laugh. We talked so much. I miss that."

"You loved him."

"But it's like she doesn't."

"Of course she does. It's just hard when your dad isn't great, you know…" Amira sighs. "Don't be too hard on her."

"She's so angry with me."

"She'll forgive you. It's a hard time for all of you."

"Yeah – I guess."

"Just promise me one thing," she says, squeezing my hand in hers. "Just promise me that if you feel the need to hurt yourself, you'll call me. It doesn't matter what time. Just call me, please."

I don't answer at first. I can't. I dig at the earth harder, making a small well, a hole in the dry crusty mud. I wonder where the worms are, whether they are baked up in this heat, or whether they are further down, hidden deep underground, safe and secure.

She squeezes my hand again. "Please, Gabi."

"I'll try," I say.

I'll try…

I want to go skating, but I avoid the park. Even though I've done nothing wrong, even though me and Amira are fine, I don't want to see Alfie. I can't forget the things he said.

Instead, I take my board and skate outside the pub for a bit, around the empty car park – up and around the kerbs and along the low wall. I even manage a few ollies on the steps that lead up to the beer garden. It's so quiet today, all I can hear is the rolling rhythm of my wheels and the soft thwacks as the board hits the ground. Each thud sends a tiny shockwave through my body, a tiny spark. I love that – the energy of the board connecting with the ground.

I am also trying not to think. Thinking just gets in the way of everything.

It's such a lovely afternoon too; the sun is warming my arms and the top of my head, but there's a light breeze. The air has a beautiful sweet smell to it: the smell of blossom and cut grass. The smell he loved. Or he used to, back in the days when we'd go out, or sit in his garden enjoying the day.

"Just breathe that in, kid! Go on – suck in the

smell. That's good air, that is. Good for the lungs. You can't beat fresh air to start the day. Makes you feel good. Makes you feel alive."

I think of him at the end, stuck indoors. Drinking more. Watching TV. Keeping the windows shut. I want to sob. Why did it have to change? Why did he have to get worse?

Stop thinking. . . Stop thinking.

I skate more quickly. I want the world to be a blur. All I want to concentrate on is my own breathing, which is getting faster and harder. This is something I can control. Only this.

"Hey! Kid! Don't go too crazy!"

I slow to a stop and look up as Dad steps out in front of me, hands on hips, a funny smile on his lips. "Sorry! I didn't mean to disturb you. You just looked completely lost in thought!"

"I'm all right. Just getting some practice in."

"You still love it, hey?" He was looking at me in a surprised way. "I hadn't realized how good you are getting."

"Well, I'm usually at the park."

"But not today?"

"Nah. Didn't fancy it."

"Fair enough." He sits down with a sigh, his hands hanging loosely in front of him. I remember the days when he used to smoke. Looking at the way he's fiddling with his fingers, I know he's dying for a cigarette now.

"You used to practise at your granddad's, didn't you?" he says suddenly.

"Yeah," I nod. "I liked it there. The patio outside. And Granddad liked to watch, especially when I first started. It was nice."

Dad nodded. "I guess we didn't show much interest in those things, your mum and me. Not enough anyway."

"It's OK," I say. I notice how sad my Dad is looking, how tired.

"It's not that we didn't care, you know that?"

"Of course."

"And I always thought we did our best by you. I never understood why you wanted to be with your granddad so much, but maybe I didn't

I didn't bother to try and understand. Does that make sense?"

I nod. "I guess. . ."

"This pub – it's become everything. I work all hours, and for what? To become a shadow in this house. To not even notice that my daughter is suffering."

"Dad – it's OK. Honestly."

"But it's not OK, is it? The pub just hasn't been doing well recently. I've had to work longer hours to make up for the staff I had to let go." He sighs. "I'm sorry I've not been around more. But I want this to work. For us. I need to get us through the tough spell."

"I should've realized," I say. "I didn't know things were that bad."

He reaches forward and takes my hand in his. "I never want you to worry about stuff, Gabi. That's my job. I feel like I've failed you."

"You haven't. . ." The words are catching in my throat.

He looks up and he has tears in his eyes. I

think for a minute he's going to pull me to him in a hug, like he used to when I was little. But he doesn't. Instead he just wipes his face with the back of his hand and sniffs loudly.

"Anyway, there's no one in the bar. I've got to get back, haven't I?"

And he marches back inside.

Only I notice his shoulders are shaking as he does.

Back indoors, I want to avoid Mum, but I think she might be avoiding me too. She is in her bedroom with the TV turned low. This morning she was still in bed when I woke up.

I go straight to my bedroom and see it straight away. A leaflet lying on my bed:

Help for Self Harmers.

A post-it note has been stuck on the front with Mum's writing across it. *Made an appointment at the doctors. 5 p.m. tomorrow.*

I sigh as I pick the leaflet up. The photo is of a pretty blonde girl with her face turned away from the camera. The stock picture for "I'm hurting and need help". I'm not ready to read this. I really don't want to, so I throw it on the desk, hoping it might evaporate in the middle of the night.

Instead I pick up my phone. I find my site, my sanctuary. There have been lots of updates. Lots of people have struggled this weekend. Also, many new members have joined – all calling out for help and advice. Some have just posted introductions, others have included pictures. The pictures do not shock me any more. I open them up with a kind of sadness, a solidarity. They all seem to cry out the same thing.

It shouldn't get to this. But it has. This is the end result. Please fix this.

My post tonight is simple.

www.hiddenscars.com

Thread: RE: Re: Grief

Hi Guys

Looks like tomorrow I'm going to the doctor's. Mum knows about my self-harm and is not happy – but I'm guessing they might be able to help, right?

I've got to try anyway.

And my mate is trying to help too.

I do want to stop. But I can't make any guarantees. I'm just taking it one step at a time.

x

I think that this will be my last post for a while. I'm not sure whether it helps being on here or not. But at least I know it's there.

I click off and choose to watch YouTube videos of skateboarding tricks instead. I've not done that for a while. I lay back on my bed and zone out, trying not to think of Granddad. Trying not to think of the admiring comments that he might have made.

Sometimes not thinking at all is the easiest thing to do.

It was my usual time. My board was under my arm; my hand was on the gate. I was here to check on him.

But I couldn't go in.

I looked at the house – at the tightly drawn curtains. At the red front door, now badly chipped with age. At the wire window above it that I used to trace as a kid – that all seemed so long ago now. A lifetime away.

I knew he was inside. He had nowhere else to go. All I had to do was walk around the side and let myself in. The side door was always open. Waiting. He'd be sitting there, watching TV, not doing much else. Rotting in his own bitter juices.

But what would be the point of me going in? He didn't want me. Mum had told me often enough. "Drink makes you loose-lipped. It makes the truth come out. It makes you say what you really mean."

He'd told me to go. He told me didn't want me any more.

I bit my lip. Then slowly turned around to go.

Just then, I saw his neighbour coming out of

his own house – the big man that had shouted at Granddad before.

"All right?" he said. He looked awkward, embarrassed maybe.

"Yeah. . ."

"Look, I'm glad I saw you," he said. "I wanted to check everything was OK. I heard your granddad shout out the other night – he does that sometimes. But I knocked on the door and there was no answer. I know he's not one for company but I wanted to make sure he was all right. Have you been in there? Have you seen him?"

I thought of Granddad when I saw him two days before – swaying and shouting. Spitting. Probably he was still angry, then – still shouting out his bitterness and hate. "He's fine," I said. "He was just drinking."

"So I don't need to worry?" He seemed relieved – he was ready to go back into his house. His lovely, safe house with the freshly painted door and potted plants on the step. "I mean, I'd normally be more bothered but he's done this before – you know. I got worried and nearly called someone and turned out

he was just passed out cold from drinking. He gave
me a mouthful of abuse that time for trying to help!"

Yeah – I could've imagined!

"No. He'll be fine," I said. "Don't worry yourself."

Some people you can't help, can you?" he said,
sadly.

"No. No you can't," I agreed.

And I walked away.

CHAPTER
SEVENTEEN

No. No. No...

I'm so sorry, Granddad. I'm so sorry...

I wake suddenly. Another dream. A flashback. I can still taste it in my mouth – there is dryness all around my teeth. I want to gag. Something heavy is clamping my chest and the panic claws through me. For a few seconds I feel trapped, until the spell breaks and I can move again. I hate it when this happens, when I wake up too fast and I can't move. It has a name. Sleep paralysis – the body's way of protecting you, stopping you from hurting yourself in dream state. But it scares me. For a few seconds at least I feel enclosed, buried in my own nasty dreams.

But it's OK now. I'm back here. I'm OK.

I wonder when these nightmares will stop – when I will start feeling normal again. I'm sick of waking up feeling the same way, remembering the same things.

My sheet and duvet are in a twisted mess at the foot of the bed. I roll out slowly and stretch my legs. Long, pale legs now covered in faint bruises from yesterday's practice. My fingers trace the outline, like marks on an apple – old blood being pressed up against my skin.

Beside me my phone is flashing its bright light again. I reach for it. Two messages are waiting for me. One from Amira:

> Hi Babe. Hope you were OK last night. Remember – call me if you need me A x

The warmth surges through me as I tap a quick reply. I thank her. She's lovely to me, I must never forget that.

The second message is from Alfie. My stomach twists. Do I want to see what he says? My thumb rubs the screen absently before finally daring to open it.

> Gabs, I've been an idiot. I'm really sorry. Come to the park this morning. Pls. I need to talk to you x

I study the words for a minute, drinking them in. Then I smile. No reply is necessary. But I will go. I do need to see him.

I walk out, past my mum's room. Her door is shut. I wonder if she's still asleep.

In the bathroom I shower. I run some oil through my curls. I pin back my fringe away from my face. I apply a little make-up, not much, but enough to make me feel fresh and pretty.

And then I take a photo. And another. I frown into the lens. I drop my gaze. I try all the angles. I want my other self to be reflected back in the shot. The one that is coping.

But every image is ugly.

Dad's on the phone to Gloria when I leave. I hear him mutter, and then he flashes me a worried look. I know he's talking about her. I just turn away and drink my juice.

Maybe I was harsh, blaming her for neglecting Granddad. But she did push him away. We could have helped him more. All of us.

But there's only one person to blame for his death.

Even though it's hot, I jam a beanie hat over my curls. I skate most of the way to the park, needing the speed and distraction. Today, I'm not interested in looking at the shops as I pass, or nosing at the houses. I just need to keep moving. If I stop, I might change my mind. I might go back. I might not face Alfie.

I see him straight away, at the base of the ramp. There are only a few people there today: some younger kids that I barely know and Dylan, who's busy doing tricks on the top. Alfie is at the base, turning his board around slowly. He is facing me and looks up as soon as I approach, a shy smile sweeping over his face. He pushes his hair back.

"You came then!" he says.

"Obviously."

"Fancy some runs or shall we talk first?"

I shrug. "I guess talk?" I turn on my board, try and look casual. "Shall we sit over there again?"

"Sure."

We move to the bench. It's weird, the atmosphere between us. It's never been like that before. I've always been so relaxed around him and now there is tension, stretched out like a rubber band. I hate it. We sit down, leaving a gap between us. Alfie is sitting forward, his board behind his legs, kicking at it.

"You were out of order," I start to say.

"I know. I'm sorry," he mutters quickly, which is annoying. I was spoiling for a proper fight.

"I'd never do anything like that to Amira, you should know that," I continue angrily. "Freddie was upset, that's all. And I was upset too."

"I know, he explained. I was a twat," he sighed.

"I was just so frustrated. I really liked you – *like* you! And I just thought you were messing me around. I lost it."

"Yeah – well. . ."

"And I'm sorry for what I said after. I was angry. I didn't mean it."

I don't say anything, but I hate the way my eyes are prickling again. Why does this always happen to me? I'll look like such a loser if I start sobbing. Instead I turn away and focus on Dylan, who's jumping really well today. I feel the itch inside me. I want to be up there with him.

"I am so sorry, Gabs. I know you're going through a rough time right now. I get that. Can we just—"

"Just what?" I'm still not looking at him. I don't want him to see my red eyes.

"I dunno. Be friends, definitely. Be more than that, if you want. You know I like you. It's your choice. You can decide what we do from now."

I watch as another kid, much younger than me, twists in the air – so high, his face pinched with pleasure. For the split second you can truly see the happiness, you can capture it in his face. It's an amazing thing. The itch is building within me – the need to be amongst the clouds.

"I want to be up there," I say pointing at the ramp.

Alfie looks where I'm pointing and then nods and grins. "OK, then."

For a moment neither of us moves – there's this awkward "something" buzzing between us. Then, just as I think he's going to get up, he leans forward. Slowly he places his hand on the side of my face and turns it towards him. Then he leans in.

The kiss is as soft as a breath. His lips taste warm and familiar, like I've known them all my life. As he pulls away, his hand is still on my face; he strokes the skin softly, sending sparks of electricity though my entire body. It's as if I'm flying again, spinning in the air, touching the clouds. I am light. I am free. For a second, just a second, the weight inside is lifted.

"I just ... I really like you. That's all," he says, a smile settling on those beautiful lips.

"I like you too. I really do."

He pulls me close. I rest my head on his shoulder and he lets his head rest on mine. This feels good.

"I'm sorry I'm so screwed up," I say. "I feel all over the place."

"Let me help you."

"Why would you want to?" I whisper.

"Because I do, OK?" he replies, his voice firm.

"OK," I say.

"We can take things slow. There's no rush at all. Seriously. I'm here for you."

"You're lovely," I say. And I mean it.

"You're lovely too," he says softly. "I just wish you believed it."

I walk home feeling different, almost.

I should be happy. I just kissed an awesome boy. My best friend is my best friend again. I should be feeling more positive.

But I'm not.

Because I still remember.

I went back. I went back and I opened the door.

Just behind me the storm was swelling. Heavy rain whipped against my back, clawing at me, trying to drag me back into its cold grip. My thin coat was already soaked right through and clung against me like a wet, useless flannel. The empty bins rattled with the force of the gusts and the gutter poured water against the wall, a relentless, murky waterfall, spilling out on to my shoes.

It was nasty, unforgiving weather that refused to end. This was meant to be the start of summer, but it might as well have been the depths of winter.

I edged through the door and into the room beyond.

The smell hit me first. Deep, dark and filthy. It settled in my throat and made me want to gag. The light was poor. All the curtains were drawn, as if the house was closing in on itself. Entering the room was like stepping into a rotting piece of fruit with its juices slipping down my throat and into my nostrils, making it hard to breathe.

I walked through the next door, gently pushing

it aside. The TV was so loud that the sound was distorting. Canned laughter bounced off the walls, mocking the scene in front of me.

Laughter. So much laughter.

I wanted to block my ears. I wanted to run.

But I didn't.

I had a question to ask.

I wanted to ask him if he meant it, about wanting me gone.

The words were on the tip of my tongue, but they lodged in my throat as soon as I entered.

I called his name. It seems silly looking back; it was obvious what had happened. But I still called his name. Still I rushed to his body. Still touched his swollen face. Oh my god, that face – the one I see in my dreams. Will I ever forget it? And the smell. Causing me to choke, to recoil. To gag.

NO! NO! NO!

He'd fallen. There was blood. He'd hit his head and by the looks of the vomit congealed around his mouth, he'd choked where he lay.

My granddad. My poor granddad.

I don't remember reaching for my phone or even dialling. But I remember the calm, clipped tone of the voice on the other end.

"... are you sure he's dead? Have you checked his airways?"

"He's been here for ages!"

"And who are you please?"

I couldn't stand this. I couldn't. I just needed to be gone. "I'm no one. No one at all. I was just passing."

I hung up then. I'd given the address. I didn't want them to know about me. I wasn't even meant to be there. Not like this.

I was no one.

Then I bent forward and saw it. The scrap of yellowing paper clasped tightly in his right hand.

The two of us, circled in a heart. Me with pigtails and Granddad with a big smile on his face.

My picture. The one that he carried in his wallet. Was it a sign? That he had wanted me there all along, that it had just been the drink talking, that he'd loved me?

I guess I'll never know for sure.

I left. And I walked.

I walked for ages in the cold wet rain. My clothes stuck to me. My shoes were leaking, feet stinging. I didn't feel a thing. I didn't cry. Not once. But those tears, they didn't go – they began to trickle inside me and slowly filled me up.

When I got back home Mum was sat on the sofa, silent, facing away.

Dad was pacing up and down, his face white and set. He pulled me to him when I walked in.

"Gabi, love – there's something we need to tell you. Something awful has happened to your granddad."

It was as if the lights inside me had dimmed. The final flutters inside of my stomach settled. I closed my eyes and let the "other me" take over. I had to. It was the only way.

"Oh," I said. "What is it?"

I opened my eyes and let them tell me.

CHAPTER EIGHTEEN

When I walk back into the pub it's obvious something is wrong. For one thing, it's too quiet. Then I see Gloria's bright yellow coat on the arm of the chair. She never comes unless it's an emergency. I've been out for about three hours and she's made it down from Manchester. Something must be bad.

The living room is in semi-darkness. On the table I see photos; they are pulled out of albums and lie scattered everywhere. From the bedroom I hear the crying. Soft sobs from Mum and the quiet voices of Gloria and Dad.

I lean forward and look at the photographs. My

heart leaps into my throat. I've never seen these before. There is a photograph of Granddad, young and healthy, standing in front of his scooter. In another he stands amongst a gang of Mods, looking cool and composed in jeans and white top. In another he has his hands wrapped around a young woman. I have to take another look. The woman is a petite blonde, pretty – just like mum, the spitting image.

I pick up one more photo. It's of Granddad and he is holding a young girl in his arms; she has blonde pigtails and a sulky face. He is smiling down at her. His face is bright with pride.

He did love you, Mum, see? He really did...

I drop the picture and see that my hand is shaking. It's a history I've never seen before – a past that had been buried away.

"She's struggling, Gabi."

I turn and see Gloria standing behind me. She looks tired and tear-stained and is holding a cup of tea in her hand. She looks at the photos and not me, as she picks up the one of Mum and Granddad. She gives a little smile.

"My poor little brother. And poor Rosie. The sad thing was, if they'd both got help, things might've been different."

"Got help?" I blink at the picture, confused.

"Oh yes," Gloria says softly, her finger carefully stroking his image. "Poor Rosie, she was so ill Looking back it's pretty obvious that she must've had post natal depression, but it was missed. Everyone thought she was coping, but quite clearly she wasn't and it all became too much for her."

"What happened to her?" I ask. "I mean, did she get treatment?"

Gloria blinks back the tears. "No one knows for sure. I'd like to think that she got help in the end. That she started again, but—"

Her words are lost as she shakes her head. I can see tears are building in her eyes again.

"And Billy – he couldn't cope after she left. He missed her too much – he didn't understand what had happened to his Rosie. He'd liked a drink before, but he started drinking then, badly. He did some bad things. Made some mistakes. In the end it didn't work out. I had to look after your mum. It was for the best."

"What did he do?" The stirring inside my stomach is increasing; a whirlpool is being created, mixing everything up. Everything I thought I knew.

I don't see Mum walk in. She must have crept in silently, padded in with bare feet. She looks like a ghost. Wild hair, red eyes, pale, pale skin.

"He told me I was evil," she says, her voice so gentle it's childlike. "That he blamed me for everything, for breaking his wife. For ruining his life. He said I looked too much like her, that he hated me for it. He said that to me every time he drank, and soon he was drinking every day. Some days he wouldn't speak to me at all. It was as if I were a devil child."

"Mum. . ." I say.

Gloria steps towards her, but Dad is there behind Mum, sweeping her up in a huge hug, his big arms supporting her. "Gabi doesn't need to hear this," he says.

"She wanted to know. She kept asking." Mum

is shaking, tears pouring down her face. "All I wanted was his love, but he could never give it. When he eventually left for good, I was ten years old. Just ten. I didn't even know where he'd gone. The next time I saw him was eleven years later, in our pub, with him begging for my forgiveness."

"And you let him back in," Gloria says softly. "Many wouldn't have."

"I didn't want to. I wanted to scream at him, hurt him like he hurt me. Tell him where to go. But I guess a part of me was still hoping he could make things right. And he promised me it'd be different. He wanted to get to know you, Gabi. And he did. He gave you what he could never give me."

"Mum..." My words catch in my throat. I don't know what to say.

"I told him he couldn't be around you if he was drinking, so he stopped. For you. He loved you enough. But not me!"

I see her pain, the rawness of her loss. The

damage that she has carried for too long. Her face has sunken in. Her lips are still moving. Her nails are digging into Dad's arm.

"He did love you," Gloria says firmly, then she turns to me. "He did. But he was ill. He couldn't see until too late the damage he had done. He tried to make it right with you, Gabi. He wanted to be there for you. I guess he wanted to prove he was a good man."

The chill is creeping up my throat again. I can barely move, barely speak. "He did..." I say.

"I should've done more," Mum sobs. "He needed our help to stop drinking, I do know that. But I couldn't. I was still so angry."

"No. No." Gloria shook her head. "You weren't to blame. He was an alcoholic. My God, I shut him out too. The trouble was he could be so nasty; he was wicked to me at times. I never forgave him for the things he did in the past – and perhaps I should've. If I'd been a better sister..."

Dad steps forward. "That's crap, Glor – you've done so much for this family."

"But not my own brother!" Gloria's voice is shaking.

"He killed himself. He drank too much and fell. No one could've prevented that," Dad says. "It's sad, but those are the facts."

"But if I'd gone round to check on him – if he'd been found earlier—" Mum says

If he'd been found earlier. . . I feel a chill running through me. My stomach is a solid mass of ice.

"I just wish I could've seen him. I wish I'd given him another chance," Gloria says softly.

I look up at her – at my aunt that I barely know. She doesn't look a bit like Granddad except that she has his kind grey eyes. I want her to make everything better. I feel I can tell her the truth about what I did, or what I didn't do. But will she ever forgive me?

"Gloria?" I say.

"What, Gabs?"

"I—"

"We should have done more!" Mum weeps again, louder this time. "It took Gabi to make me see. It took my own daughter to show me what a bitch I'd become. And I'm sorry. I'm so, so sorry."

And suddenly she's on me, sweeping me up in a hot teary hug. I hold her shuddering body against mine. I look over at Dad, who is standing awkwardly beside us. I want to pull him towards me. I want to tell him what I've done, that I need him, but his eyes are avoiding mine.

"I'm sorry," Mum whispers into my hair. "I miss you, Gabi. Please, please can we make things better?"

"Yes, Mum," I whisper and I hug her back.

Holding her this close is good. It is so, so good.

If he'd been found earlier.

But inside the ice still swirls and whirls.

I'm back in the bathroom, my safe place. Locked in and enclosed. My head is against the cool wall. I am concentrating on my breathing and trying so hard not to think. Trying so desperately hard.

In this room, all I can hear is Mum's gentle sobs and Dad's soothing words from behind the closed door. I think of those photos scattered on the table. I think of all the buried memories and the future that has been lost.

I think of that one photo. Of Granddad, so different. So happy. Of his lovely face as he looked at my mum as a baby. Things could've been so different for both of them. For all of us.

I think of Rosie, my nan. Where did she go? Mum talks about her as if she's lost, someone swallowed up in the past, caught up in the mists somewhere, suspended in space and time. Is she waiting for us? Or is she reunited with Granddad again? Are they both happy now?

Was he just waiting all that time, getting through the days until he got her back?

Why weren't we enough?

I squeeze my eyes shut. My head throbs and the sour bile taste is rising in my throat again. I wrap my arms around my body and sit still, trying not to move. I know I'm shaking and I don't know how to stop.

I could tell them. I could tell them now that this was all my fault.

That I could've saved him. Gone in and checked on him like I told the neighbour I had.

That I should've saved him.

And that eventually I was the one to find him – *like that.*

Maybe I could tell them. Not yet, but soon. I know that I can't keep this stuff inside me for much longer. It is bursting out of me.

It just hurts too much.

The icy fingers are wrapped around my tummy. The weight of my tears are still inside, dragging me down. Pinning me to this position. Making me helpless, lost, scared.

I blink. Hold my body tighter.

I think of Mum, holding me close after so long. I think of the chance that we have to make things right.

I think of Dad and the startled pride in his eyes as he watched me skate.

I think of Alfie, and a sudden warmth drifts through my bones, deep into my muscles. I see his smile, feel his kiss again. A different ache settles inside me.

I think of Amira, of her holding my hand, stroking my skin. Understanding me like no one else really has.

I'm so confused, so muddled, it's like my brain is wired all wrong.

I want to make the right decision.

I do.

But I need this pain to go.

I can't stand it.

It is breaking me apart.

Please help me.

Please.

In front of me is my phone, and my razor.

In front of me the screen glows. I can call Amira. It'll be so easy. She is waiting for me.

Like always.

I can pick up the blade.

Or I can call my friend.

I reach forward and make my choice.

AFTERWORD

Whilst *Damage* is a work of fiction, its roots are based on the experiences that I have worked with first hand and the research I have undertaken.

Like many, my understanding of self-harm was fairly limited. Growing up, I had a few blinkered views about the types of people that tended to self-harm and the reasons why they would do so. I didn't understand the motivation, nor did I understand the process. Maybe I didn't want to know. This was a failing on my part and this viewpoint soon changed.

When I began my work in a secondary school, I quickly moved into a role within child protection, and every case of self-harm was referred to me. I had to attend training sessions on the subject, which helped my understanding a little. I also had to read and research the subject more to help those who were harming. I spent a lot of time just talking to the individuals that were going through this. It soon became quite clear that each case, although very unique, had one underlying theme – the individual was feeling some pain or frustration inside and needed a way of letting some of it out. Rather like letting out a little gas from an over-inflated balloon, self-harm provided this release – albeit for a very short period of time.

And then the guilt and pain sank in. It was a sickening and addictive pattern of self-abuse.

Helping those that self-harmed wasn't about dressing the wound and telling them never to pick up the blade again – they knew this already. It was about addressing the pain and internal hurt. It was about talking and getting to the root cause of the feelings behind the need to inflict that damage in the first place.

In my novel, Gabi is suffering from grief and this is something I could identify with. Only two years ago, I lost my Dad and I knew how the pain of loss could strike you hard, how it could sit heavily inside you and feel like it had nowhere to escape. I was lucky. I could cry – I could let some of that emotion out. But Gabi couldn't. Her pain was trapped, contained – and that led to her self-harming.

In *Damage*, Gabi also visits websites and forums to help her reach out to others that might understand her situation. I researched websites that are currently in operation. And whilst I'm aware that some are very frank and can be triggering, it cannot be denied that many young people also find solace and support in these sites. As with everything, it is about striking a balance

Please also remember that self-harm is not limited to the young, it can affect anyone at any time. It should not be a stigma. It should not be something that is hidden away in a bathroom, or bedroom and not discussed. I believe that openness and discussion can help us all to increase our understanding and empathy and will help us to help each other. And, if you have been affected by any of the issues raised, I would please ask you to contact the websites or phone lines provided at the back of this book. Help is there. I promise.

We need to look after each other, not judge. We need to listen to each other, not preach. And we need to keep reading, talking and understanding.

More information on self-harm can be found
from the following organizations:

YOUNG MINDS
www.youngminds.org.uk

HARMLESS
www.harmless.org.uk

THE WISH CENTRE
www.thewishcentre.org.uk

RETHINK
www.rethink.org

MIND
www.mind.org.uk

Or, if you would like to talk to someone,
you can contact the following organizations
24 hours a day.

CHILDLINE

www.childline.org.uk

Phone: 0800 1111

THE SAMARITANS

www.samaritans.org

Phone: 116 123

ACKNOWLEDGEMENTS

This is always hard, as I have too many people to thank. I always worry (as worriers always do) that I will miss someone important out.

It goes with out saying that I thank Tom, for his unending support, wonderful hugs and endless cups of tea. I am also thankful l that I have two crazy, insightful children, one nutty puppy and a grumpy cat that keep me laughing (and screaming occasionally). Thank you for making my life much brighter.

I am grateful to my agents, Stephanie and Rebecca,

for putting up with my daft questions and making everything so much easier. I'm thankful to my fantastic team at Scholastic, in particular my editor, Gen, for her expertise and skills in helping *Damage* become the beauty that it is today.

I would like to thank my wonderful, supportive and ever-so-slightly crazy family for keeping me motivated. And also my fantastic group of friends who keep me grounded, sane and happy. Manatees will always make smile.

Thank you to Pete Boxall for his help with skating lingo in Damage (I really had little clue) and to my fab beta readers.

Thank you to my patron school Glenthorne High School and for every other school I have visited in the last year. These visits continue to inspire me.

An all mighty huge thank you to the wonderful bloggers and librarians who have supported my